Sherlock Holmes

and

the Mystery of

the Faceless Corpse

[Being another manuscript
—along with an appended postscript—
found in the dispatch box of
Dr. John H. Watson, in the vault of
Cox and Co., Charing Cross, London]

As Edited By

Daniel D. Victor, Ph.D.

Book Eleven in the Series,
Sherlock Holmes and the American Literati

Hardcover 978-1-80424-609-2
Paperback ISBN 978-1-80424-610-8
ePub ISBN 978-1-80424-611-5
PDF ISBN 978-1-80424-612-2

Published by MX Publishing
335 Princess Park Manor, Royal Drive,
London, N11 3GX
www.mxpublishing.co.uk

Cover design by Awan

Also by Daniel D. Victor

Cruel September

The Seventh Bullet:
The Further Adventures of Sherlock Holmes

A Study in Synchronicity

Sherlock Holmes and the Shadows of
St Petersburg

The Literary Adventures of Sherlock Holmes,
Volumes 1 and 2

"Sherlock Holmes and the American Literati":

The Final Page of Baker Street

Sherlock Holmes and the
Baron of Brede Place

Seventeen Minutes to Baker Street

The Outrage at the Diogenes Club

Sherlock Holmes and the London Particular

The Astounding Murder at Cloverwood House

Sherlock Holmes and the Pandemic of Death

Sherlock Holmes and the Case of the Fateful Arrow

Sherlock Holmes and a Tale of Greed

Sherlock Holmes and the Hearthstone Manuscript

Acknowledgments

Once again, many thanks to Tom Turley, who not only corrected my facts and strengthened my story, but also supplied me with enough inspiration to make the necessary changes. My thanks as well to Judy Grabiner who never seems to tire of reading my work and offering worthwhile suggestions. Thank you to Sandy Cohen for his consistently intelligent insights and recommendations. Also, for sharing her knowledge and encouragement, my deep appreciation to Charlotte Gunvor Thorkildsen, Library and Archives Assistant at London's Natural History Museum. (Whatever errors I might have made regarding the Museum are my own, not hers.) Finally and most significantly, I wish to thank my wife, Norma Silverman, for her never-ending supply of sage advice, good counsel, and infinite patience.

A note on the text: In addition to the title of the book, all chapter and section titles, headnotes, and footnotes were supplied by the editor.

Dr. Rodrigues Ottolengui
(1861-1937)

Chapter One

An Exchange of Letters

Reading detective stories . . . help[s]
to increase the analytical quality of the mind . . . .
-- Rodrigues Ottolengui
Quoted by Douglas Green
*The Battered Silicon
Dispatch Box*

Unlike the relationships Sherlock Holmes and I have developed with a number of other Americans of distinction—Henry James, Anna Katherine Green, and the young Frank Norris come to mind—neither Holmes nor I have ever met Dr. Rodrigues Ottolengui, a respected dentist noted not only for his writings in the dental field, but also as an emerging purveyor of romantic fiction.* It is nothing short of ironic, therefore, that my recent epistolary exchanges with the man served to entangle Holmes and me in one of the most gruesome murder investigations in which the two of us have participated.

What is more, in addition to the monstrous nature of the crime itself, the calendar creates its own cause for concern. Very much a part of the following account is the prevailing date: it is nearing the end of February, 1891, as I take up my pen, and I fear that I may

---

* See Ottolengui's *Conya: A Romance of the Buddhas (1890)*

7

lack the time to complete the entirety of this narrative before the start of some grand police mobilisation with which Holmes has become involved and which may interrupt our activities regarding the case generated by Ottolengui. But I get ahead of myself. Allow me to return to the beginning.

A most curious letter from New York dated the fifth of this month, but which required a fortnight to reach me, precipitated our involvement in the ghastly business. It was then that the unknown Dr. Ottolengui (at least, unknown to me at the time) posted a singular request seeking my help as a man of science in securing an artist for his analytical writings on insects.

With nothing greater in mind than fulfilling his entreaty, I had no reason to anticipate the untoward consequence that a search would evoke—a consequence so chilling that in leading me to a fashionable house in the northwest of London, it revealed not only a horribly disfigured corpse but also any number of possible purveyors of murder.

Dear Dr. Watson [the letter began],

Allow me to introduce myself. By profession, I am a dentist. I was born in Charleston, South Carolina, but live in New York, where, augmenting my practice, I have invested a great deal of time writing about dental science. [*] *In addition to my wife, May,*

---

[*] See Ottolengui's *Methods of Filling Teeth - An Exposition of Practical Methods* (1891).

and my various writings, my interests include taxidermy and the study of Plusiinae, *those delightful creatures most normal people call moths. With that study in mind, I'm hoping to publish a paper on my capture in Prospect Park here in Brooklyn of the geometrid moth,* Brotis vulneraria.

Which brings me to the point of this letter. I am in search of an accomplished individual to illustrate my latest examination of those insects and have come to learn that some of the most skilled of such artists reside in London. [*] *To find such a talent, I have sought the help of your countryman, George Hampson* [†] *an expert entomologist whose book,* The Lepidoptera of the Nilgiri District, *describes the moths he encountered in India. Unfortunately, gone unanswered is the letter I sent to him at the Department of Natural History in the British Museum where he volunteers his expertise.*

You may rightly ask why I am telling you all this. The answer is simple. You see, in addition to my scientific endeavors, I am also an enthusiast of forensics who hopes to create mystery stories of my own someday. As a consequence, though I am primarily interested in writing fiction, I have closely followed not only your riveting accounts of the factual investigations involving Sherlock Holmes but

---

[*] In the years to come, Ottolengui would rely on American artists like Edna Hyatt Beutenmüller (1872-1934).
[†] Later, Sir George Francis Hampson, 10th Hampson Baronet of Taplow.

also those less dramatic reports of his cases furnished by the public press.

In particular, I refer to that business surrounding the Baskerville affair of two years ago, which I read about in the papers.* Although the criminal elements obviously intrigue me, entomologist that I am, I must also tell you how fascinated I am by the references to the Vandeleur moth, the creature so named for the fellow in East Yorkshire who first described it.† While you justifiably know the man by his alternative names and murderous intentions, I—with no thought of minimizing his nefarious nature—recognize him as an outstanding entomologist. And to think that you have actually seen his small museum with its glass-topped cases full of mounted butterflies and moths!

As medical professionals, I am certain that you and I share the same respect for the medicative sciences—not to mention our similar interest in solving crimes. With so much in common, I hope I might convince you to do me the honor of tracking down George Hampson at the British Museum and discovering just why my letter to him has produced no response.

---

* Watson's own version, *The Hound of the Baskervilles,* would not be published until 1902.

† It was Rodger Baskerville II, also known as Jack Stapleton, who discovered a subspecies of the Emperor moths commonly found on the Yorkshire moors. The subspecies in question has been identified by Sherlockian Tom Turley as *Saturnia vandeleura.*

I eagerly await your reply.

Sincerely,
Rodrigues Ottolengui, M.D.S.

I do indeed recall the butterflies and moths on Dartmoor—Cyclopides, I remember labelling them in my notes, always flying about and darting among the flora. Moreover, like the next man, I remain particularly vulnerable to kindness and flattery, especially when such compliments come from a kindred spirit—not only a member of the healing profession but a successful writer as well. In point of fact, it was Ottolengui's congenial nature that prompted me that very day to take up his request and, I am pleased to say, to achieve success almost immediately.

Happily, there was no great mystery concerning the reason Ottolengui's post to George Hampson went unanswered. In a word, it never reached him. As it turned out, though the American's letter was properly directed to London, I soon discovered that George Hampson does not work at the Department of Natural History in the British Museum in Great Russell Street, Bloomsbury, as Ottolengui believes.

Rather, despite Hampson's publications for that institution, I was informed by an officious clerk in the personnel department that the entomologist himself can be found at the similar-sounding Museum of Natural History in Cromwell Road, South Kensington, where, thanks to his financial resources, he does indeed work gratis. At least, Ottolengui got the volunteer-part right. As to why his letter to Hampson had not simply been forwarded, I never received an explanation.

The next day, a wintry Friday morning, I completed in a little under an hour the invigorating two-mile walk to the museum from our home near Norfolk Square in the Paddington district. I found George Hampson with no difficulty. Eager to help facilitate my search in locating an artist for Ottolengui's study of moths, Mr. Hampson referred me to one Clive Watney-Banks, his deputy in charge of the listings for such artists.

"Bearded chap," Hampson told me. "Quite capable. Also a volunteer. Lives with his niece—his ward, actually—in a small villa in St. John's Wood. But be forewarned. He has a bit of a temper when riled."

Unfortunately, Mr. Watney-Banks was working at home that Friday rather than at the museum, so I had no opportunity to speak with him. But in for a penny, in for a pound, I decided that Sunday afternoon, with none of my patients to see and my beloved wife, Mary, off for a few days' visit to an aunt in Cambridge, I would pay the gentleman a visit and—his temper notwithstanding—pass along Ottolengui's request for the name of available entomological artists. Mission decided, I wrote to Ottolengui of my intention to meet with Watney-Banks and promised to keep the American apprised of my progress.

I lay the blame for the convoluted tragedy in which I would soon become entangled on my failure to schedule the visit in advance. I had no trouble finding the house that cold Sunday in St. John's Wood.

Fortunately, there was no cricket at nearby Lord's. The year before marked the opening of the Thomas Verity Pavilion, which replaced the previous structure destroyed by fire. At twenty-one-thousand pounds, the new cricket ground brought with it ever-increasing crowds, but on this day the sidewalks remained relatively free of pedestrians. In fact, compared to the traffic of Baker Street or Paddington, the tree-lined lanes of St. John's Wood—though less picturesque with their winter branches lacking leaves—appeared refreshingly quiet.

My destination, the home of Clive Watney-Banks, the deputy to whom Hampson directed me, stood in a quiet little turning off the Wellington Road just past the St. John's Wood Church Gardens and about a mile from the Regent's Canal—a waterway whose importance in this narrative will soon become evident. The Watney-Banks property, set in the midst of a broad greensward and encircled by oaks, is appropriately called Woodlawn House.

Relatively small with gardens in the rear, Woodlawn House resembles another fancy home in the vicinity with which Holmes and I are familiar—Briony Lodge in Serpentine Avenue. That fashionable *bijou* villa served as the scene of a most remarkable adventure four years previous involving Irene Adler, the female adversary to whom Sherlock Holmes would always refer as "*the* woman." (I might add that my account of the business, which I have titled "A Scandal in Bohemia," is scheduled for publication in July.)

As for Woodlawn House, it is fronted by a paling fence of dark-stained wood some six-feet high and partially concealed by a thick, dark hedge. The fencing includes a black, wrought-iron gate supported by a pair of red-brick gate-posts with the name, *Woodlawn House*, spelled out in brass block lettering on the left-hand side. The approach includes a short flagstone path leading to the cupola-covered porch. With its white façade, flat roof, and black wooden shutters, the villa looks quite inviting.

Feeling luck in my corner, I knocked on the outer door. No sooner did I do so than I heard the Chubb lock unlatch. The door opened, and a well-dressed, young footman appeared. From him I learned that I had arrived in the midst of a celebration, which in spite of the chill was taking place in the garden—the festivities commemorating the occasion of Watney-Banks' ward-and-niece, Olivia, upon reaching her majority.

"Actually," I said undeterred, "it is Mr. Watney-Banks, not his niece, I am hoping to see."

The footman shook his head. "Alas, sir, though Mr. Watney-Banks did attend the luncheon, I'm afraid he is currently working inside the house. His instruction to me was quite specific—he was not to be disturbed. I dare not ignore his orders."

With my altruistic mission for Ottolengui in mind, I was about to ask if I might nonetheless dare pose to Mr. Watney-Banks the briefest of questions concerning the Museum of Natural History. But no sooner did I open my mouth to speak than a loud gunshot suddenly intervened. I started in surprise.

"Not to worry, sir," smiled the footman. "A shooting competition is going on in the garden. Come. As you are an acquaintance of Mr. Watney-Banks, I'll show you."

Though the footman had got our relationship wrong, I followed his lead. It took but a minute to pass round the house where I was relieved to discover there was indeed no cause for alarm. Upon the flagstones, a good distance beyond the food tables, canvas canopies, and a small greenhouse, a circular target had been placed. A group of leafless plane trees served as protective backdrop behind it.

Positioned near a wooden summer-house some fifty yards away from the target was a fashionable quartet of contestants—two young men and two young women—each one (or so it appeared to me) a representative of the leisure class. The women wore long woollen coats and turban hats; the men, corduroy trousers and jackets—one, an abbreviated, navy-blue overcoat; the other, a brown Norfolk shooting jacket. All four held shiny silver pistols which they carefully kept pointed downward at the flags.

Soon I would learn the names of the contestants: Watney-Banks' niece, Olivia, the young woman with the wisps of yellow hair spilling out from beneath her hat; Roland Frothingham, the gentleman in the short, navy-blue coat, Olivia's friend from childhood and now her beau; Eugenia Frothingham, Olivia's companion and Roland's sister; and Reggie Folger, the fellow in the Norfolk jacket, whose eyes were fixed on Eugenia.

The footman had left me standing next to another young man. David Belford, he called himself. Like the Folger chap but less fashionably dressed, he too seemed interested in a young woman, the servant called Rose Greener, who, attired in uniform black dress and white apron, was watching the competition from behind a nearby serving table.

Later, Olivia was presented the opportunity to explain her interest in guns: "A few years ago," she would say, "I attended Buffalo Bill's Wild West Show when it was here in London at the Queen's Golden Jubilee. Annie Oakley enchanted me—so much so that I decided to learn to shoot. My friends took up the hobby as well, and we're quite competitive within our little circle. We call ourselves 'The Shooters Club of St. John's Wood.' We all use the same kind of American guns that Annie did—a silver-mounted, .44 calibre

Smith and Wesson Model Number 3. We each have our names engraved on the handles, and all four of us are expert shots."

Though not a member of the club—nor for that matter of their social standing—David Belford told me that he liked his friends' guns so well that he had bought one of his own, save that his was neither silver-mounted nor engraved.

As it so happened, the competition I found myself observing that Sunday afternoon had come down to a final contest between Olivia and Roland.

Since wagering has always been an interest of mine, I asked Belford, "What are the stakes?"

"Not money," he smiled, "and not even simple satisfaction. You see, Rollo and Livy have been stepping out together for quite some time, and before the shooting contest, he told her that following the competition, he wanted to ask her uncle for permission to marry her.

"'Only if you win,' Livy laughed.

"'Spot on,' Rollo said."

With stakes so high, I watched with fascination as the drama unfolded. It was Olivia, handsome in face and form, who first stepped to the line marked in chalk on the flags. As she calmly stretched out her arm, closed one eye, and took careful aim along the six-inch barrel at the circular target, her cool composure made me think yet again of Irene Adler.

I had little time to ponder such similarities, however, for she steadied her arm, fixed her gaze, and fired. The blast echoed through the trees and her arm recoiled at the shock. Nonetheless, she immediately stood tall and marched over to the target to evaluate the result. "A quarter-inch off the bull's eye," she frowned and moved well away from the shooting range.

With a confident smile, Roland Frothingham, square-jawed and keen-eyed, shrugged off his short jacket and tossed it on a nearby chair.

"Why don't you get a coat that fits, Rollo?" Reggie Folger shouted.

The young man ignored the gibe and windmilled his arm to signify his freedom. All business now, he stepped up to the shooter's mark, his intensity signalling to all the magnitude of this final shot. Before the hushed crowd, he raised his shiny revolver in the direction of the target, sighted down the barrel, took careful aim, held his breath, and squeezed the trigger. A loud report—and immediately the young man headed off to see the result.

"Bull's eye!" he shouted to Olivia amidst wild cheers and the acrid smell of gunpowder. "I'm off to see your uncle," he announced, pausing only to reload and slip into his jacket before making his way to the house.

"Rollo, wait!" Olivia shouted, but he was already through the door.

David Belford smiled broadly at Rose Greener though it seemed to me that Rose herself had an anxious look about her.

It took but a few moments for Roland to emerge. Gesticulating wildly, he appeared locked in an argument with a black-haired, bearded man I assumed to be Clive Watney-Banks. "Never will I allow my niece to become involved with a Frothingham," the latter shouted, his cheeks florid with rage. "Never with a family as corrupt as yours, a family with death on their hands. Never! Devil take you all!"

Finished with his execrations, the truculent Watney-Banks turned towards the house, but Roland was still holding his pistol. "You can't speak that way about my family," Roland exclaimed and, slowly raising the gun, pointed it at Watney-Banks who, at the sound of the threat, had turned round to face his accuser.

I cannot say with any certainty that the young man was actually going to shoot the uncle of his intended, but at that very moment Olivia came running towards Roland. Just as she knocked his arm upward, the silver-mounted revolver fired, and the bullet flew off in one direction and the pistol in another, coming to rest at the feet of Watney-Banks. Revellers shouted and screamed, and Roland scrambled after his gun, but it was Watney-Banks who got to it first. Though the older man looked pale, he managed to stoop and pick it up, and all the defeated Roland could do was march out of the garden, his face distorted in rage.

"You all saw that miserable cretin try to kill me!" Watney-Banks shouted. "He'll not be getting this gun back to try again." With those determined words, he staggered towards the house.

Reggie Folger hollered at his back. "There are other people who have guns, you know, people who think you're very wrong to stand in Olivia's way."

"I'll have my dog on you," Watney-Banks spat out.

"You should be ashamed of yourself," Eugenia addressed the older man. "You're the host here. I could shoot you myself!"

Olivia, holding Reggie back, managed to quiet Eugenia. Then Olivia told everyone to leave. When she got round to me, she demanded, "Who are you?" I told her I had come to speak with her uncle about his work, but she told me to leave anyway.

Clearly recognising that this was no time to be asking Watney-Banks about people who could paint Ottolengui's moths, I followed her instructions. My query concerning such an artist could be put off until the next day when I would get a locum to attend my morning surgery and hope, however naively, that the family tensions would have subsided by then.

The last words I heard at Woodlawn House were Olivia Watney-Banks' instructions to Rose Greener, the woman who—much more than a servant, I would soon discover—acted as cook, maid, and housekeeper all at the same time. On this occasion, Olivia told her to round up the crew hired to set up for the festivities and have them strike the tents and party tables.

Despite the dramatics that followed the shooting match, I remained committed to my goal of securing the name of an artist for Dr. Ottolengui. Thus, the very next day I travelled back to St. John's Wood. Unable to improve upon the account I sent to him concerning my ill-fated re-appearance at Woodlawn House, I present in full my letter detailing the terrible events I witnessed there.

23 February, 1891

My Dear Ottolengui,

One can only shudder at the happenstance your search for an artist has uncovered. Irony is too benign a word for the deadly scene into which a would-be crime-writer like yourself innocently propelled a chronicler of detection like me. Murder will out, they say, but only time will tell if that is the case.

As I wrote in my previous letter to you, Ottolengui, with the hope of finding an artist to illustrate your work, I intended to pay a visit to Clive Watney-Banks, the deputy of your associate, George Hampson. Indeed, just yesterday I made the short trip to Woodlawn House, the deputy's residence. Unfortunately, a birthday celebration that included a shooting-match and its highly-charged aftermath thwarted my attempts to speak to the man, and so, ignoring a snowfall that had covered the ground in the night, I returned to his home early this morning.

Imagine my surprise when, upon exiting the hansom, I observed a black police van parked by the kerb in front of Woodlawn House. Avoiding the various heaps of snow as I made my way to the outer door, I recalled the previous day's shooting competition—not to mention the subsequent argument—and wondered into what I might be getting myself.

I was surprised again when, after I pulled on the bell, the door was opened not by a footman in formal attire, but by Inspector Stanley Hopkins. One of the youngest of the Scotland Yard detectives, he was wearing his customary tweed like a uniform beneath his overcoat.

"Dr. Watson," said he equally surprised, "don't tell me Mr. Holmes is here as well. I myself received the report not more than thirty minutes ago."

"No," I replied, wondering to what report he was referring. For my part, I explained that I was

simply there seeking professional information from Clive Watney-Banks.

The inspector shook his head. "I'm afraid your questions for Mr. Watney-Banks will have to go unasked. It is he, you see, who is said to have died."

"Died?" I repeated, immediately recalling the heated argument I had witnessed between Watney-Banks and his niece's suitor that ended the day's shooting. "Whatever do you mean?"

"Come in," said Hopkins. "I've just finished speaking with Miss Olivia Watney-Banks, the niece—adopted daughter, really." He indicated the young woman seated on a red-damask settee at the side of the room.

So taken was I with the unexpected appearance of the inspector that I had failed to notice the blond-haired woman who only yesterday had reached her majority. Dressed in a dark-blue frock, she sat with her hands clasped and a stoic expression. Ensconced next to her was a large, fawn-coloured mastiff. He was called Hengist, I would soon learn, named for the heroic Anglo-Saxon leader.

Hopkins pulled me aside and spoke softly— presumably out of respect for the young lady. "I've had only a quick look in the library at the corpse, and it's not a pretty sight. I don't yet know what happened, but the niece told me about the incident with the gun at a garden party yesterday, and—"

"I'd been there as well," I interrupted. *"I was trying to speak to Watney-Banks, but never got the chance. That's why I came back today."*

"So, you saw this Roland Frothingham draw his pistol and fire a shot."

"I did."

"Well," said the inspector, *"I'll take a statement from you later, and as soon as I leave here, I'll be sending officers to West Hampstead where she told me this Roland Frothingham is staying."*

As he spoke, the inspector turned to look at the nearby hallway which one could assume led to the library. "Listen, Doctor," Hopkins said, obviously impatient to begin his work, "I need more facts. Whether you were here yesterday or not, the police surgeon is late, so why not act in his stead?"

Having worked as a surgeon in the military and therefore familiar with the ghastliest of wounds, I felt quite capable of fulfilling the policeman's request.

"You were at my party yesterday," Olivia said to me when Hopkins informed her that I was going to examine her uncle's remains. But before I could offer an explanation, she got to her feet, turned, and led Hopkins and me through the hallway and towards the library though neither she nor the dog would go in.

It was a cold room we entered; the fire was out and a window was open. Yet it was the sickening smell of burnt flesh that overpowered everything else save the horrific image I shall never be able to put out of my mind.

Clad in an open, burgundy-coloured dressing gown and white, linen night-ware, the body of Clive Watney-Banks, the poor girl's uncle—the man I had come to consult on your behalf, Ottolengui—lay on his side upon the floor, his head a blackened mass of charred flesh still lying on the grate. The fire had rendered his features indistinguishable. In a word, he had no face.

The embers below the iron hearth-grate upon which the scorched head rested had extinguished. Thus, whatever had happened to the unfortunate fellow that had caused him to collapse head-first into the fire—a seizure or heart-attack, perhaps—must have occurred hours before.

As part of the standard procedure, I felt for his pulse, which I knew to be non-existent. As I told Hopkins, the man was mercifully dead. I got the policeman's permission to pull the body out of the fireplace, but when I rolled the corpse onto its back on the half-moon hearth rug, I discovered a new horror. The side upon which the dead man had been lying was drenched in blood, his linen mottled with scarlet stains. The red pool had originally been concealed by the body, but once having turned him over, I could see a vast quantity of blood covering the hearth and now seeping onto the rug.

"It's not just the fire," I told Hopkins. "There's lots of blood under him." A bit of exploring provided the source. "He's been shot," I said and indicated the wound. "Here in the left side."

Hopkins looked startled. "Shot, you say?" Immediately, he looked about the room, finally fixing his eyes on the floor. "There are bits of glass on the carpet. The shot must have come through the window." Turning to examine the open sash window, he observed, "Why, there's a bullet hole in only one of the facing panes, not in both as one would expect if at the time of the shot the windows had been positioned as they are now."

Whilst Hopkins was contemplating the window, I opened the dead man's dressing gown and began to probe the wound.

"Clearly," Hopkins said, lowering the upper sash, "the window was closed when the shot was fired. Someone had to have come into the room after the shooting and raised the bottom sash."

"My word," I exclaimed, not paying attention to Hopkins. "The man's linen contains a single bullet hole, but there are actually two gunshot wounds here."

It took but a moment for Hopkins and me to reach the same conclusion: Assuming Sherlock Holmes to be in England, it was time to contact my friend.

Rest assured, Ottolengui, that I shall continue to keep you apprised of how this investigation develops. In the meantime, if I were you, I would search elsewhere for that artist you're looking for.

Yours sincerely,

John H. Watson

The American's reply required another fortnight to reach me; in fact, it arrived after most all of the drama had ended and I was in the midst of composing this very narrative. Ottolengui's response was short and simple.

Dr. Watson,
I look forward to reading your account of the matter. Your report may be just the impetus I've been seeking to begin my career as a crime-writer. Nonetheless, I am indeed sorry for getting you involved in this terrible business.
Good luck.

On this occasion, he had signed his name "Rod."

Chapter Two

Murder Most Foul

In seeking to entertain is it not best
to offer something out of the common?
Something a little different from
the dull routine of daily existence?
--Rodrigues Ottolengui
The Crime of the Century

Not only has Sherlock Holmes blanketed in a cloak of secrecy his activities for the final months of 1890 and early '91, but he has also failed to supply me with a schedule of his frequent returns from the Continent. As a result, I have no way of predicting his appearances in London.

It goes without saying that since my marriage two years ago and Mary's and my subsequent move to Paddington, Holmes and I have been forced to modify the logistics of our friendship. Why, we see each other so infrequently that between the final few months of last year and the start of this one, I recorded a mere three cases in which the two of us worked together.[*]

What is more, I—the man whom Holmes has called his personal Boswell—was reduced to having to learn alongside common readers of the daily press the

---

[*] In the biography, *Sherlock Holmes of Baker Street*, William S. Baring-Gould suggests that Watson refers to "The Adventure of Wisteria Lodge," "Silver Blaze," and "The Adventure of the Beryl Coronet."

news of Holmes' current work for the French government. To be sure, his letters to me from Narbonne and Nimes in late-January revealed that his stay in France would be lengthy, but despite the rumours that his current investigation is related to the theft of an unnamed national treasure from the Louvre, he continues to insist that he cannot discuss the nature of the assignment.[*]

Fortunately, the message that Inspector Hopkins and I sent to Baker Street that Monday morning found my friend at home and prompted his immediate trip to Woodlawn House.

I met Sherlock Holmes at the outer door. Though prepared for the cold in his Inverness cape and deerstalker cap, he continually peered this way and that as if to assure himself that he had not been followed— an insecurity, I should add, that I am unaccustomed to seeing him display.

"Let us step inside," he said, laying a hand on my arm. "It's safer all round that way."

Once within the confines of the entrance hall, I asked him if he was in any danger.

"Not yet, old fellow," he said reassuringly. "The French enquiry offers no problems, but I am also working in collaboration with the Yard on a massive case. It is the reason that I have been required to make so many returns to London; in fact, it is the reason your message found me at home. Though in our ever-changing universe, one can never divine complete success, I predict with some confidence that in a matter of weeks, Scotland Yard will have set its trap in motion,

---

[*] One can't help wondering if the assignment in question might have inspired Vincenzo Perrugia's notorious theft of the *Mona Lisa* from the Louvre in 1911.

and a vast network of criminal enterprises will be shut down." *

Beyond this tantalizing titbit, Holmes has refused to go. "I've already had a few small victories in the investigation," he assured me. "One at the start of the year, another a few weeks later, and yet another in the middle of this month. But as you well know, dear Watson,"—here he held up his index finger, a teacher highlighting a lesson—"even minor victories can provoke grand retaliation."

Now I am no stranger to the growing list of malefactors with whom Sherlock Holmes has battled. One recalls the desire for dominance in London's underworld by self-fancied masterminds like John Clay and Professor Moriarty. Indeed, both have posed ominous threats to my friend.† What is more, Holmes revealed that such concerns remained very much top-of-mind.

"During the past few weeks," he said, "I've escaped a number of dubious accidents that seemed clearly planned—a falling roof-tile, a runaway horse, a loose step outside 221B—but nothing I can prove that was premeditated. Worse, as the police close in on the villains and the noose tightens, I expect such attacks to increase and be less disguised."

"You must take care, old friend," I said.

---

*Unbeknownst to Watson at the time, the "massive case" Holmes referred to was the Holmes-orchestrated probe into the illegal undertakings of Professor Moriarty.
† See Watson's accounts in "The Red-Headed League" and *The Valley of Fear* respectively.

He offered a brief smile. "I shall watch my step until the Yarders make their final move—sometime in late April or early May, I should imagine."

Although Holmes has been frightfully frugal about the details of the case, he speaks with a foreboding that suggests an all-encompassing commitment, a commitment that I sense will inevitably demand my involvement. Strong enough is my concern, great enough do I feel the sense of urgency, that I am compelled to complete this narrative before whatever is to happen actually occurs.[*]

In terms of the murder at Woodlawn House, I reported to Holmes the confrontation I had witnessed at the garden-party between Roland Frothingham and the late Clive Watney-Banks. In light of the two gunshot wounds suffered by the deceased, I also informed Holmes of the so-called Shooters Club of St. John's Wood, describing for him in particular the major personages in the drama of the previous day. My account included the apparent relationships between the dead man's niece, Olivia Watney-Banks, and Roland Frothingham, Eugenia Frothingham and Reggie Folger, and David Belford and Rose Greener.

Holmes also asked for descriptions. When I began with Olivia's blond hair, however, he said, "I'm more interested in their sizes. One cannot miss the footprints in the snow outside of the house, and I would very much like to match steps to perpetrators."

---

[*] Readers will note that the mysterious trip to which Watson alludes led Holmes to his infamous confrontation with Professor Moriarty at the Reichenbach Falls in Switzerland on May 4, 1891.

I began with the women: Olivia was the shortest, Eugenia the tallest, and Rose somewhere in between. Of the men, Belford stood tallest, then Folger, then Frothingham.

"Excellent," said Holmes. "Let us now proceed to the body."

Holmes frowned when, upon entering the library, the putrid smell hit his nostrils.

"Mr. Holmes," said Hopkins turning away from the fresh air at the open window in order to greet my friend. "It's good to see you back safe and sound."

"Not the most fortuitous of circumstances," Holmes replied.

"Agreed, but I would be most appreciative of any insights you might have to offer in relation to this terrible crime." Hopkins was a young detective who astutely regarded Holmes as a mentor.

Placing his cap and cape on the nearby wing chair, Holmes surveyed the open window and its solitary bullet hole. "Closed when the bullet was fired," he said. "Opened sometime thereafter."

Sherlock Holmes now looked round the room. In particular, he noted the location of the two doors, the fireplace, the black-leather couch and a blanket of Black Watch Tartan wool folded tightly upon it. Next, he bent down to examine some dust on the carpet and immediately cast his glance upward. Neither Hopkins nor I had thought to look in that direction earlier, but we now stared up at the ceiling and could not fail to note the small rent in the plaster responsible for the dust on the floor.

"It is possible," I observed, "that the bullet which came through the window travelled upward and buried itself in the ceiling."

Holmes stared at the marred surface above us and then at the window. "A tenable view, Watson."

"And thus," Hopkins added unnecessarily, "it is one bullet that did *not* bury itself in the body of Clive Watney-Banks."

Holmes snorted at the obvious conclusion. "At least two shots were fired," said he matter-of-factly. "Unless it is magical, a single bullet cannot strike a person, then defy the laws of gravity, turn ninety degrees, and fly upwards into the ceiling."

"But there are two wounds," Hopkins said. "So how many shots are we talking about? Three? And fired by whom? And from where? For that matter, the unfortunate fellow might conceivably have been struck yesterday by that bullet at the garden party that Watson reported. Such a hit would account for one of the wounds."

Sherlock Holmes surveyed the distance between the open window and the floor, then leaned out over the sill and looked down. After pulling himself back in and standing upright, he said, "The space from the window to the floor is about two feet, but it's closer to five feet from the bottom of the window to the ground outside. Even if the window were closed, a shooter holding his pistol at eye-level in the garden would have a fairly straight shot through the glass pane at a target in the library. In any case, the two wounds are a fact we should keep among ourselves until we learn more details about the killing."

As he spoke the words, I recalled the firing stances of the two members of The Shooters Club I had witnessed aiming their pistols the day before—two shooters, Olivia and Roland, who felt deeply wronged by her now-dead uncle.

Finally, Holmes turned towards the body lying on its back close to the hearth where I had moved it.

"I pulled him out of the fireplace," I reminded Holmes, "and turned him on his back. That's when I discovered he'd been shot in the side—twice."

Holmes nodded. "Not a robbery," he said, pointing to the thick, gold wedding ring still encircling the dead man's fourth finger of his left hand. He gave the ring a tug. "In any case, it's too tight to pull off easily." Still looking at the hands of the corpse, he muttered, "Hello, what have we here?"

Holmes raised the right hand of the dead man, which was curled into a fist. Opening the fingers, he extracted a small gold locket, its fine chain trailing afterward like a lazy flow of water. With his magnifying lens he examined the cover and a moment later read aloud what he had found there, "'*JF to AF.*'" Snapping it open, he showed us the likeness of a blond-haired little girl. "A young, Olivia Watney-Banks, I presume."

"Missed that," I confessed. "I was more concerned with the wounds."

Holmes waved off my oversight. Slipping the trinket into a pocket of his waistcoat, he crouched low and moved to study the entire body. First, he examined the two bullet wounds in the victim's left side—clearly, entrance holes—and then, employing his lens, he carefully scrutinised the charred remains of what was left of the poor man's head. "In some places the flesh is entirely burnt off," he observed grimly.

I had witnessed the same.

"Enough," Holmes announced at last, and rising abruptly, unfolded the Tartan blanket that lay on the nearby couch, and covered the body. "Let us see where that other door leads."

Hopkins and I followed Holmes to the portal in the side wall. He opened it quickly, and we immediately found ourselves staring into the bedroom of Watney-Banks' niece. In a nod to femininity, light-blue wallpaper accented with small yellow flowers covered the walls, but like the library the chamber felt cold. It was easy to see why. The fireplace stood back-to-back with its duplicate in the library, and the two shared the same chimney. Given the horror in the adjacent hearth, one could understand the desire to avoid a fire that day.

Walking in unannounced as we had done presented the possibility of a most embarrassing situation, but fortunately the young woman, wrapped in her wool coat, was sitting at her desk by a window. To say we startled her is an understatement. In a paroxysm of surprise, she slammed shut a drawer and sprang to her feet. At the same time, she tried hiding an envelope inside her coat—but not quite quickly enough to conceal from us a stamp and address on the envelope's face.

What is more, as she rose, a tiny object dropped silently from her lap to the carpeted floor. I knew Holmes had noted it, and a glance at Hopkins told me he had as well.

"I am Sherlock Holmes," my friend said to the surprised young woman. "Excuse our interruption. We had no idea where this door led." As he spoke, he bent over whatever had fallen. "We finished our work in the library," he continued and without any explanation picked up the object and placed it in his pocket.

Olivia stared straight at him, ignoring his action. "I found the body," she announced coldly. "I walked into the room, smelled the stench, and—despite the cold—opened the window to let in fresh air. Only when I turned about did I see my poor uncle."

"So," noted Hopkins, "the window was originally closed—just as we thought. That explains the bullet hole in the single pane."

"It must have been quite the shock," I said, "finding him like that."

"I was angry with my uncle—the way he had treated Rollo that afternoon. You were there, Doctor. You saw. But never could I wish such a horrible fate upon anyone."

Whilst she was speaking, I looked round the room. Although the wash basin was an obvious *accoutrement* for the young woman, the same could not be said for the long wire bore-brush lying on a blue towel at its side. Military man that I was, I recognised the stiff bristles for cleaning a pistol-barrel.

"Not to put too fine a point upon it, Miss Watney-Banks," Holmes said, "your uncle was shot, and I understand you and your friends have created a shooting group—'The Shooters Club of St. John's Wood' I believe you call yourselves. One assumes, therefore, that you own a gun."

"Why, yes, of course," she replied, "but what does that have to do with anything? I certainly didn't shoot my uncle."

"No," said Hopkins, "but, your friend Roland Frothingham is also a member of the club, and as I understand it, he almost did just that in the garden yesterday."

Olivia Watney-Banks showed no emotion at the charge. "I'm sure *he* didn't shoot my uncle either," she said definitively.

"That remains to be seen," replied Hopkins.

The young woman grimaced at the policeman's comment, and we recognised it was time to leave her room. Before exiting, Holmes paused to ask a final question. "Might we look through the rest of the house?"

She nodded her approval, and Holmes, Hopkins, and I went off to survey the premises.

We began on the ground-floor in the bedroom of the dead man. Moving directly to the closet, Holmes proceeded to riffle through the jackets.

"What are you looking for?" I asked.

"Since there was only one bullet hole in the night dress, perhaps the non-fatal shot occurred when he was wearing a suit."

"You're referring to the bullet fired at him from the garden," I said.

"Quite so," murmured Holmes in the midst of making a quick inventory of the closet. With no success, he turned to the drawers of Watney-Banks' bureau. Unlucky again, he was forced to conclude that he could find no evidence to support his conjecture.

Next, we mounted the stairs and looked round the upper storey. Holmes paced each room and corridor as if he were measuring them and seemed to take special note of the closets on the ground floor and the armoires in the rooms above.

Only when Holmes signalled the completion of the task did we quit the house, exiting out into the cold through the French windows in the villa's dining room. Standing in the spot I had occupied but the day before at the birthday gathering, I realised that in retrospect the murder of the man I had come to see on behalf of Dr. Ottolengui seemed not as unpredictable as one might think. For as I was soon to understand, that final gunshot of the previous afternoon did more than reflect the anger of a singular young man. Rather, it served to suggest the lethal undercurrents that were churning within the minds of all the principal attendees in the garden.

Chapter Three

The Footmarks in the Snow

What I know are but trifling facts;
what you know, on the contrary,
is perhaps of great importance.
                    --Rodrigues Ottolengui
                    "The Duplicate Harlequin"

No sooner had we stepped into the garden than we were struck by the chill. From late November to early January, temperatures had been exceptionally cold. There was little sunshine breaking through, and snow and ice covered much of London.

Though the weather has recently turned less severe, one cannot predict with any certainty when icy spells will again descend upon us from Scandinavia, and the three of us were prepared to meet the chill— Inspector Hopkins and I in overcoats; Sherlock Holmes in his Inverness cape and deerstalker; and on all our hands, kid gloves.

It was just such an open gloved-palm that Hopkins extended when we paused outside the house. "The locket, if you please, Mr. Holmes," he said. "Evidence."

Holmes fished the charm and its chain out of a pocket and dutifully turned it over to the inspector.

Placing the pendant in his waistcoat, Hopkins said, "Now, Mr. Holmes, I'll also thank you for whatever it was that you picked up from the floor in Miss Watney-Banks' room."

This time it was Holmes who held open his gloved palm. In it lay an empty bullet casing. "Forty-four calibre," he added and turned the shell over to the policeman.

"Thank you again, Mr. Holmes," Hopkins said, placing the shell in the other pocket of his waistcoat. "And don't you worry. Sooner than later, we'll also get a look at that letter the young lady tried hiding away."

Upon the completion of the exchange of evidence, I announced with a sweep of my arm, "This is where the garden party took place yesterday."

Despite the missing tables, tents, and shooters' target, the grounds appeared much as they had the day before. Such an observation, however, could not include the snowfall of the previous night and what looked to me like an indecipherable *mélange* of footmarks interrupting the whiteness blanketing the ground.

"The snow has laid down a sufficiently thick carpet that will facilitate our investigation," Holmes explained. "Rose Greener told me that last night's flurries began just before five and ended about half nine. Footprints made in the snow after it stopped falling should appear sharp and clear. But fortunately for us, there wasn't enough new snow to cover the earliest prints. They will look less distinct because fresh powder will have partially filled them."

"The more snow within the footprint," I reasoned, "the earlier the pedestrian traffic."

"Quite so," said Holmes.

Hopkins and I were about to march out into the grounds when Holmes put out his arm to block our progress. "Gentlemen," said he, "I will thank you to remain here whilst I study the landscape. There is much to be read from these footprints, and I would not have all three of us mucking about and ruining the tracks."

"But, Holmes—" Hopkins was about to protest.

"See here, Inspector, the flags leading to the front door are already a mess with too many people, including ourselves, coming and going. We need to protect the integrity of what's left of the area. I won't spend much time out there. But I assure you that I shall return once I comprehend the meaning of the footprints here in the garden." With those words, he was off, careful to avoid stepping into the prints he was examining.

Sherlock Holmes began at the green house. "A few footprints here, but nothing of interest," he announced after only a few minutes. Then he turned, slowed his pace, and advanced in the direction of the sand-coloured summer-house. As he angled forward in his dark Inverness and tweed deerstalker, he stood out against the white backdrop.

Looking down all the while, Holmes detoured only slightly by way of the two black, wrought-iron gates that led to the road, the larger main entrance and a smaller side gate. Twice he stooped to pick up something, but he was far enough away so neither Hopkins nor I could see what he had collected.

When he finally reached the summer-house, an airy, octagonal structure separated into a pair of equal areas by a chest-high partition of lath-and-plaster, he entered through its open portals and remained inside for about ten minutes. Thanks to the glassless windows and lack of doors, we could watch Holmes as he moved about.

For a moment, however, he disappeared from view, bending low behind the interior wall. A few moments later, he stood up again and passing through the rear exit of the summer-house, marched off in the direction of the distant Regent's Canal. It was then that I noted another metal gate which I had not seen before leading towards the plane trees that lined the waterway.

Just then, an impatient Hopkins tapped my arm and nodded to the barely visible portion of the path leading from the front door of the main house to the road. Upon it, I saw Olivia Watney-Banks approaching the main gate. A dark fur coat now blanketed her, and a red scarf covered her blond hair. When she reached the sidewalk, she turned left and marched off.

"The letter she hid from us," I said to Hopkins. "I'd wager she's off to post it."

"Right you are, Doctor. I was thinking the same."

"Why, she must have been waiting for us to leave the house, so she could go out and send it on its way. If only we could find out to whom it is addressed, let alone its contents."

Hopkins assumed his most erect posture. "I'll follow her," he said. "The post office is nearby. I fancy she'll leave it there for pick-up." With a brief wave, he strode off in the same direction taken by the young woman.

A half hour passed before I saw Holmes plodding back towards me. I told him that Hopkins had gone off to follow Miss Watney-Banks and the letter, and then I asked what he had discovered.

Sherlock Holmes pointed to the ground, and as he delineated the distinctions among the footprints, I began to recognise the differences.

"The smaller footprints belong to women," said he. "Whilst I can't identify with absolute certainty to which women, one can still offer reasonable hypotheses. The smallest prints originate from the house, so we may logically conclude they were made by the smallest of the ladies, Miss Watney-Banks. Though the ones that come from the road are larger, the stride is small and thus presumably also made by a woman—most probably, by a friend and no doubt frequent visitor."

"Eugenia Frothingham."

"Eugenia then. Olivia's prints lead from the main house to the entrance of the summer-house where they are joined by a man's larger prints that come from the side gate.

"The earlier prints by Eugenia also come from the side gate and proceed to the summer-house. Because Eugenia's prints were almost obliterated by the snowfall, one may conclude that in anticipation of a meeting between the man and Olivia, Eugenia arrived at the summer-house before the two of them did. She then hid behind the inner wall in order to hear their conversation without being seen."

"But why do you say she hid? How do you know that she simply did not *join* their conversation?"

"Because Eugenia's footprints access the summer-house from a side entry." Holmes pointed to the structure. "As you can see from here, to allow the air to circulate, the summer-house has no doors or glass windows. It is a design clearly intended for hot weather, but one that nonetheless allows cold air—and more importantly for our purpose, snow—to enter as well.

"The few small prints of a single person within the summer-house—Eugenia, in this case—suggest little movement behind the inner wall; thus, one may conclude that she hid there so as not to be seen but where she could undoubtedly hear the conversation taking place between the later arrivals who had come through the front entrance together—presumably, Olivia and, perhaps, Eugenia's amour, Reggie Folger."

"Strong words, Holmes. But you can't be sure. What makes you offer up Reggie instead of Roland as the man meeting with Olivia? It is Roland, after all, who seems to be Olivia's intended."

Holmes sighed. "I believe the footprints are larger than Roland's, but, really, dear Watson, I ask you—as a man of the world—what better time for a young woman to eavesdrop on her male friend than when he meets with another woman?"

I must confess that it was sound reasoning; I could not argue with Holmes' logic.

"After the meeting," Holmes went on, "Folger left the summer-house to return to the gate, but as a jumble of prints reveals, he was attacked by a dog—presumably, the mastiff. To be sure, there are large dog prints throughout the landscape, but where I was looking, they merged with the man's. Judging by the increased length of his strides—he ultimately ran off to the side gate to make his escape.

"Olivia, on the other hand, left the summer-house and headed toward the Regent's Canal behind it. I followed her tracks along the water's edge for some fifteen minutes. Near the Macclesfield Bridge they disappeared."

"But she's come back to the house."

"Yes, Watson. A newer set of her footsteps does indeed lead back from the canal, though a still-later set of a small man's prints also originates there—in this case, as you posited, no doubt Roland Frothingham's. Like the others, these prints also lead to the house—only by a different course, offering no sign of any kind of meeting between the two of them. The second set shows that the man moved along the outside of the house, past the windows of the library where Watney-Banks was shot, but it's not clear whether the man actually entered the house."

"Just what does all this mean, Holmes?"

"One can't be certain, of course," Holmes said, but reaching into a deep pocket beneath his Inverness, he added, "I did, however, find a pair of interesting objects in the snow—this one, just outside the summer-house." Much to my amazement, he produced a silver-mounted revolver. The name engraved on the handle read *Eugenia Frothingham*.

"Another member of the St. John's Wood Shooting Club," I said. *The murder weapon?* I wondered silently. I also wondered what else my friend had turned up. "You mentioned a *pair* of interesting objects, Holmes. What else did you find?"

With a quick smile, he reached beneath his cape again and this time withdrew a second silver-mounted pistol. It appeared identical to the first, save that on its handle was engraved the name *Reginald Folger*. "I found this one near where the dog attacked the fellow. There was blood in the snow, so Folger must have been bitten. One bullet has been fired from each gun. Folger may have shot at the dog, as may have Eugenia."

"You could be right, Holmes," I said, "but they might also have shot at Clive Watney-Banks through the window, one bullet hitting him, the other lodging in the ceiling. They both threatened him. Why, for all we know, that meeting between Olivia and Folger was to arrange the murder of her uncle. With Watney-Banks out of the way, the pair could quash any investigation into the disagreement which took place in the afternoon between Olivia's uncle and Roland, a fellow Shooters Club member, let us not forget."

"Perhaps," Holmes mused.

"Why, for all we know," I went on, "Folger actually did shoot Watney-Banks at the *fête* but didn't kill him, and when Olivia found that to be the case, she completed the job."

"We need to learn more," Holmes said. "I assume that Miss Watney-Banks is still on her mission to the post office. We should still have time to re-examine her room."[*]

Sherlock Holmes and I entered Woodlawn House through the French windows, and Holmes led the way to the room of Olivia Watney-Banks. He immediately made for her desk and the drawer which both of us saw her shut when we had burst in unannounced.

It took but a moment for Holmes to open the drawer and remove the woman's silver-mounted Smith and Wesson. Like the revolvers Holmes had found in

---

[*]One wonders whether the American mystery writer, Carolyn Wells, was thinking of Sherlock Holmes' 1891 analysis of the footprints in the snow—or Ottolengui's fictional recreation of it in *A Conflict of Evidence* (1893)—when in her novel, *The Clue* (1909), two characters belittle the kind of reasoning exhibited by Holmes: ". . . In detective stories, there's always that light snow which had fallen late the night before. . . . and there's always some minor character who chances to time that snow exactly, and who knows when it began and when it stopped."

"Yes, and then the principal characters carefully plant their footprints, going and returning—over-lapping, you know—and so Mr. Smarty-Cat Detective deduces the whole story."

the snow, this one too bore its owner's name on the handle. Holmes spun its cylinder, observed the chambers and sniffed the barrel. "Very recently cleaned and reloaded—no doubt, just before we made our earlier dramatic entrance. I assume you saw the bore-brush near the wash-basin. It was lying on a towel, suggesting the bristles were still wet."

"If Miss Watney-Banks had indeed planned to shoot her uncle," I reasoned, "it follows that she would have also planned to eliminate any evidence that might incriminate her. It makes perfect sense that such action would include cleaning her pistol."

"Indeed, Watson, but it would make more sense for her to have cleaned the gun last night directly after the shooting and not wait until the morning when strangers like ourselves might accidentally walk in on her."

There remained more in the desk drawer, however, than just the pistol. With a look of determination, Holmes pulled out a mahogany box. In it were a number of sealed pasteboard cartons containing .44 calibre bullets. One of these cartons was open and held spent casings.

Holmes furrowed his brow. "That woman remains one step ahead of me. She can easily claim this box was sitting on her desk and that, like the other used-shells inside it, the spent casing she obviously saw me pick up had merely fallen out when she was cleaning and reloading her revolver at some other time. Nothing suspicious at all."

"Quite a clever girl," I remarked, wondering if Olivia Watney-Banks' sharp mind and superb figure suggested to Holmes the other woman from St. John's Wood who had also managed to stay one step ahead of him.

The sound of horses interrupted our conversation as the coroner's van arrived in the front of the house. The authorities had come to convey the body of Clive Watney-Banks to the morgue for autopsy. Holmes replaced the pistol and box in the drawer and the two of us moved into the sitting room in time to watch Rose Greener open the outer door and direct the two attendants to the corpse in the library.

Minutes later, the men passed us, manoeuvring the body—a white sheet having replaced the plaid blanket Holmes had laid on it earlier—through the front doorway and out towards the road. Drawing aside a curtain, Holmes stood at the window where I joined him, and the two of us watched as the men gently eased Watney-Banks' body into the rear of the police van.

No sooner did the van pull away from the kerb than a hansom came to a quick halt in the very same place. The blond hair of Olivia Watney-Banks was clearly visible through the side window of the cab, but the features of a shadowy figure seated next to her were not.

A red-headed, clean-shaven stranger in sea-faring togs—blue serge trousers and a pea-jacket—exited the far side of the carriage. I reckoned his age in the thirties. Hefting a bulky canvas bag onto his shoulder, he hurried round the hansom as best he could to help Olivia step out. Once she had done so, the cab drove off, and the two arrivals entered the house.

"Mr. Holmes, Dr. Watson," Olivia said, "may I present to you my cousin, Charles Watney-Banks, whom I've only just met. A chance meeting, really. It was getting dark in town, and I hailed a hansom. As we approached Woodlawn, I saw a stranger on the sidewalk struggling with his bag. Since he seemed to be coming here, I offered him a ride. He introduced himself, and it was then that we discovered we are cousins."

"Quite the twist of fate," I said.

The woman's face reddened. "My uncle used to talk about his son—my cousin—who had run off at a young age. I've only just broken the news to Charles about his father. I also told him that you were detectives trying to find out who is responsible."

I offered my condolences to the young man. At the same time, I thought to myself: *Ill-timing for the return of the prodigal son.*

Holmes was less tactful. "Cousins, you say. Yet the two of you have never met."

Charles set his bag on the ground. "If you must know," he shrugged, "I've never been close to my family. My mother died when I was eleven, and by the time I was twelve, my father had sent me off to Bedford House in Oxford. Oh, I began my schooling well-enough, but the regimentation didn't appeal to me. When I was thirteen, I was told that I would have to stay there the year round, so I decided to run off.

"Whatever money the family has comes from the tea trade my father's father was part of. Such business never appealed to me. No, it is the sea that has always beckoned, and luckily I managed to talk my way on board a Merchant Navy ship as a cabin boy. That was years ago, and I've sailed round the world. Though I sometimes thought about returning to London, long trips to China and America interfered with my plans. But then I recently arrived in Marseilles, and I decided that at last—since I was so close—it was finally time to come back."

"Marseilles," murmured Olivia. "I've been told that I went to Paris as a little girl with my mother, but I don't remember such a trip."

"Oh, it's true," Charles said. "My father told me about the journey since he accompanied the two of you."

"Why was that?" Olivia wanted to know.

"I—I can't really say," answered her cousin. "In any case, I don't consider Woodlawn my home. When I was born, we lived in Hampstead. It was only after my father had bundled me off to Bedford House that he moved to St. John's Wood. I've never been here before. What an inauspicious time to arrive. What an awful coincidence."

Another coincidence. Holmes and I exchanged glances, certain we both shared the same thought: *Such coincidences are hard to believe.* It was as if I could hear Holmes talking into my ear: "The stranger who arrives in the wake of a crime, Watson, discovers that suspicion lags not far behind."

Charles Watney-Banks expressed an understanding of our concerns. "I have anticipated your doubts," said the young man. "You are investigating a murder. You have every right to be suspicious." Producing a wallet from his trousers, he extracted from it a packet of weathered papers. "Letters from my father to me when I was at school," he said, handing the collection to Holmes. "I trust that they will confirm my identity."

As Holmes examined the yellowed envelopes, the fellow added, "I hope they're legible. I've read them often over the years, and they're not in the best of shape."

I looked over Holmes' shoulder and saw that the block letters were addressed to *C. Watney-Banks in care of Mr. J. H. Thorogood, Bedford House School, 130, Walton Street, Oxford,* and appropriately postmarked some twenty years before.

Holmes carefully slid out a fragile page. As he opened it, one could see the paper coming apart at the folds. "Dear Charles" it began, and a quick perusal proved it to be typical of the missives a father might write a young son who was off at school: *How are you? How do your studies go? How's the football?* The other letters were much the same.

Olivia leaned in to have a look. "That's my uncle's handwriting," she said approvingly. "Wonderfully neat."

"Sorry for doubting you," I said as Holmes handed the letters back to their recipient. Still, as we made our way into the house, I could not help thinking that this so-called tar did not speak like a sailor. Nor did he exhibit the callosities or the sun-beaten skin one associates with those who spend years before the mast.

Moments later, we heard a knocking on the front door, and Olivia ushered Inspector Hopkins into the sitting room. Instinctively, he regarded Charles Watney-Banks with caution, and in front of the two cousins he said nothing of his attempt to locate the letter Olivia had gone off to post. He did, however, have some new information to impart to her.

"I stopped in at the office of your family's solicitor, Basil Jenkins," Hopkins told her. "I should assure you that he was quite reluctant to share the contents of your uncle's will, but given that I was a policeman, Mr. Jenkins did provide me with the general contours of your uncle's final wishes. In a word, Miss Watney-Banks, Woodlawn and all his holdings go to you."

Olivia took a step backward in surprise. She put her hands to her mouth in an expression of shock. From our surroundings, I could sense that there was money in the family, but judging from the limited staff at the house, not as much as one might expect.

Holmes and I both looked at her cousin Charles. He was the son of the dead man, after all—the person one would suppose most likely to inherit the estate. But his expression remained blank. There appeared no sign of disappointment, no sign of the dashed expectations a commonplace crime-writer would posit as a motive for murder—in short, no reason at all for him to have had cause to hasten his father's death.

"I know what you're thinking, gentlemen," the fellow said. "You're detectives. But, please, put away your suspicions. As you can tell from my past history, I was never close to my father, and I certainly have maintained no great expectations that I would be remembered in his will. I can only assume that upon running away, I forfeited any chance of an inheritance. In a way, I am pleased to be disinherited. It clears me of the charge of wanting my father dead so I can acquire his savings."

"Actually, Mr. Watney-Banks," Hopkins said, "your father did attach a codicil. He requested that, in the event of his son's ever arriving at Woodlawn, your cousin should grant him whatever generosity she might feel appropriate."

Olivia smiled broadly upon hearing of the faith Clive Watney-Banks had in her. "Although I don't require my late uncle's encouragement to vouchsafe hospitality towards you, Charles," she said to her cousin, "you're more than welcome to stay here. For that matter, gentlemen," she added, turning toward us, "we don't have a large staff here at Woodlawn, but I can offer you rooms for as long as you need to conduct your investigation. No one wants it concluded more than I." With a wry smile, she added, "We keep the dog outside at night to frighten off intruders. You gentlemen don't have to worry about Hengist."

Holmes surprised me by readily agreeing to the arrangement. When I recalled his desire to avoid the recent threats against him, however, his desire to avoid returning to Baker Street made sense. Though I was quite ready to sleep in my own bed, with Mary in Cambridge I too decided to accept the invitation.

"I must report to the Yard," said Hopkins, but turning to Holmes and me, he added, "May I suggest we take dinner together, gentlemen. I have some matters to discuss with you."

Assuring Olivia that we would return following our meeting, Holmes and I joined the inspector for a meal at the Duke of York, the popular pub not far from Woodlawn House.

Surrounded by dark-wood-panelled walls and ensconced at a table on banquette seats, Holmes and I faced the policeman. Consistent with Holmes' worries about recent attacks, my friend insisted on facing the doorway so he could keep an eye on whoever entered the room.

"What news, Hopkins?" Holmes asked amid the low din of patrons.

"Quite a bit, actually, Mr. Holmes. All to the good, I believe."

My friend smiled. "Pray, tell us what happened. Watson reports that you were last seen marching off in the wake of Miss Watney-Banks."

The inspector nodded. "I followed her to the nearest post office where one might have expected her to leave that letter to be mailed. I don't mind admitting, however, that I was surprised to see her walk right past the place and carry on to a boarding house. In it resides"—here Hopkins consulted his small notebook—"one David Belford."

"The young man *not* in the Shooters Club," I recalled. "I stood next to him yesterday at the garden party."

"The same, Doctor. As best I could make out, she spent but a quarter hour with him in the sitting room and then hailed a cab."

"Which provided the opportunity," interjected Holmes, "for Miss Watney-Banks to discover her cousin, the sailor, on his way to Woodlawn and offer him a ride."

"Quite right, Mr. Holmes. In any case, as you can well imagine, I faced a dilemma. Do I follow the lady—presumably back to her home—or do I wait across the road from Belford's boarding house to see if that young man should make a move?"

Holmes leaned forward. "Since you arrived at Woodlawn more than a quarter hour after the young woman did, Hopkins, one may conclude that you made the prudent decision and followed Belford."

"Yes. Actually, it was quite undramatic. He simply left his lodgings and walked to the post office. The young woman must be naïve enough to believe that, if she was being followed, whoever was following her would continue to do so, leaving Belford to act as her agent free from detection. I don't know what she told him regarding the letter, but as he walked down the road, I did see him put a hand inside an inner pocket as if to reassure himself that whatever he was carrying was still there."

"A keen observation," Holmes said. "Never wise to underrate Scotland Yard, eh, Watson?"

I could not be certain that I heard the sarcasm in Holmes' voice. It was simpler to query Hopkins about the facts. "What happened at the post office?" I asked the inspector.

"Well," Hopkins replied, "once Belford departed, I showed my credential to the clerk and, whilst assuring him I had no intention of interfering with Her Majesty's mail, I demanded a look at the envelope Belford had posted."

"And what did you learn?' Holmes asked.

"The envelope was addressed to Roland Frothingham in care of the central post office in Dover."

"Dover!" I exclaimed. "A traditional point of departure."

"I view it," said Hopkins, putting both of his hands on the table, "as a traditional point of *escape*— which is how it came to pass, gentlemen, that I telegraphed the Dover constabulary. I told them to place a man in the central post office first thing tomorrow morning and detain whoever it is that comes to collect the letter with Frothingham's name on it."

"Good thinking," I said.

"Quite so," Holmes agreed. "I'm sure you'll have a report for us tomorrow on the fruit of your labours."

"So one hopes, Mr. Holmes. So one hopes."

With the probability of a positive outcome before us, we enjoyed our sherry as best one could in the midst of a murder investigation; the hearty serving of roasted lamb and potatoes that followed allowed us an additional diversion from any talk of the case. Holmes and I spoke vaguely about our future trip to the Continent, and Hopkins regaled us with word of a dramatic cricket match featuring Middlesex he had attended not long ago at nearby Lord's. After the meal, we hailed a cab, which deposited Holmes and me at Woodlawn House and then went on to deliver Hopkins to Scotland Yard.

Holding candles before us, Holmes and I climbed the stairs behind Olivia, the new mistress of her late-uncle's domicile. "Your room is above the master bedroom where Charles is, Doctor," she said as we followed her along the hallway. "Mr. Holmes, yours is above my own."

In front of our respective doors, we watched the light from Olivia's candle as she descended the stairs and disappeared in the darkness.

"It's been quite a day, eh, Holmes?" I said once we were alone.

"Quite," he agreed. "A peaceful night's sleep would be much appreciated."

"Amen," I muttered as I entered my room, and yet I knew that I still had some business to complete. Having assured Dr. Ottolengui that I would keep him abreast of the day's events, I felt obligated to send him an account before going to sleep. It was the least I could do for the man who had started me off on this sad adventure.

It was well past midnight by the time I completed my letter, the same letter (the attentive reader will recognise) that appears near the start of this narrative. I planned to post it the following day.

Chapter Four

Unanswered Questions

An opinion is dangerous.
One is so apt to endeavor to prove himself right,
whereas he ought merely to seek out the truth.
--Rodrigues Ottolengui
The Phoenix of Crime

I awoke with a start. Just past two in the morning, I heard noises—sounds of someone walking about, perhaps moving a piece of furniture or carrying a bulky object. I could not be sure, and I certainly felt there was no cause for going next door and waking Holmes. Even so, I could not sleep. Believing that whatever I heard had originated below my room, I dressed, lit the candle at my bedside, and tiptoed down the stairs.

Blackness shrouded the corridor I entered, and beyond the few feet illuminated by my candle, I could see nothing. At least, remembering Olivia's assurance that Hengist remained outside, I could eliminate the fear of being attacked by the dog—although in truth the thought never left my mind.

I inched forward cautiously, then paused to listen. At first, all seemed quiet. But wait—did I not just detect footsteps within the master bedroom a few paces down the corridor? Since I could not be certain, I soon found myself in front of the room directly below my own—the chamber originally belonging to the late

Clive Watney-Banks and bestowed only today upon Charles by his cousin.

Unless I were going mad, it now sounded as if footsteps were coming from my own room, and I actually hastened up to the first floor to check. But as certain as I was that someone was walking about, I discovered no one; all was as I had left it. So I quietly trekked back down the stairs to where I had previously been standing—in front of the room now belonging to the freshly-arrived cousin.

As one would expect so late in the night, the door was closed. But if, as I believed, I had correctly located the source of the strange noises, one would have to conclude that someone inside must be moving about. Despite the lateness of the hour, I took the chance and rapped lightly on the door. There was no response. I knocked louder, still to no avail.

Determined to get to the bottom of this small mystery—perhaps the man was simply in so deep a slumber that he did not hear my knock—I dared turn the knob and open the door. Like Diogenes with his lantern, I held the candle high and peered round the room. It was empty. Nor did it appear that the bed had been slept in or a fire begun in the hearth. In a word, there was no sign of the new arrival to Woodlawn, Charles Watney-Banks.

Where the man had gone, of course, I had no idea, but I was intent on discovering what this fellow was up to in the middle of the night in a house which he had entered for the first time that afternoon. Once the candlelight showed me that the hinges of his door appeared on the outside, indicating that the door opened into the hall, I formulated a plan. From the dining room that lay just a few steps away, I commandeered a bow-back chair from the table.

Returning along the corridor to Charles' door, I leant the chair against it, carefully positioning the top of its back under the brass doorknob. Next, I carefully straddled the seat in the tilted chair and, determined to wait until this newly-found cousin returned, I extinguished the candle. In my strategic position no one could enter or exit the room without disturbing me—even if I fell asleep.

That I do not believe I did so during my vigil makes what happened all the more bizarre. For not long after the early sun penetrated the ground-floor lace curtains and thereby illuminated the hallway, the door began to rattle.

I quickly got to my feet and removed the chair, allowing the door to open. Much to my surprise, Charles Watney-Banks emerged.

"Dr. Watson!" he exclaimed upon seeing me standing outside his room, chair in hand. "What are you doing here? I couldn't open my door."

"Maybe it was locked," I suggested though I could not conjure an excuse for why anyone would want to keep him penned in. "I—I heard noises," I added rather feebly. "Thought it best to keep watch."

Charles nodded, retreating into his room, and I, feeling foolish, replaced the chair in the dining room. Upon my return to Charles' doorway, I did manage a glance inside the room. Strangely, the bed now appeared as if it had been slept in. During that quick look, I also saw in the daylight what I had not discerned with the candle—that Charles' room, like Olivia's, had a second doorway. Hers, as we had learned earlier that day, led to the library; his, I now observed, to the sitting room.

To reassure myself that the second door would account for one's ability to be absent one moment and present the next, I rushed to the sitting room where I made a startling discovery—not only was the door locked, but the key rested in the lock on the sitting-room side. Unable to imagine how Charles could have got in or out, I remained as much in the dark as I had literally been during my late-night watch.

Though the door leading into Charles' room may have been locked, it did not prevent the hum of his voice from reaching me. In truth, I could make out no words, yet the tone sounded soft and friendly. It took a moment or so for me to realise that I was listening to Charles as he spoke to the mastiff, Hengist.

Obviously, Rose Greener, the housekeeper, had let the creature indoors, and upon wandering into Charles' room, it made a new friend. Hengist, despite the alleged attack on Reggie Folger conjured by Holmes, appeared a trusting soul. At the same time, there seemed a sincere ring to Charles' voice, as if he were used to conversing with animals.

Minutes later, Olivia joined the group. If anything, the voices sounded more muted than when Charles spoke to the dog. Not long thereafter, the two cousins, both in mourning black, walked down the hall together to the dining room.

Well aware that I heard no more strange noises once I had left my room that night, I decided not to inform Holmes of my nocturnal adventures. I saw no point in offering him the opportunity to tell me I was dreaming.

In fact, the tone at breakfast was quite sombre. When I joined Holmes, Olivia, and Charles at table, I said nothing. Since neither cousin had anything to say and Holmes remained silent as well, I assumed he intended the quietude to generate some sort of revelatory conversation. So far, at least, his strategy had failed.

In her role as cook, Rose Greener prepared simple meals. Rashers of bacon and scrambled eggs were the morning staple, along with strong coffee. As no footman was present, Rose also had to answer the pull of the bell that was just then chiming at the outer door. The ringing summoned her to the entry hall, and within a few minutes, Inspector Hopkins strode in. We were sampling our coffees at the time, and Hopkins, nodding at Holmes as if the policeman had news to impart, took a seat next to him.

Holmes and I continued drinking silently until after a few more awkward moments, Olivia stood up. "Please excuse us," she said. "Charles and I must make plans for Uncle Clive's funeral. I've been informed that the inquest will take place tomorrow and that if no obstacles arise, the service can be scheduled for Friday."

Holmes and Hopkins joined me in getting to our feet at the departure of the pair. Rose, however, continued to hover, refilling our cups, straightening the dishes, folding the napkins.

"Leave us the coffee pot, Rose," said Holmes. "And please bring another cup for Mr. Hopkins. Then you can go. We have important business to discuss with the inspector."

Once the housekeeper had departed, Holmes himself poured the coffee for the detective. Hopkins looked about to be certain that we were truly alone, and then, after taking a sip, informed us of what the police had been doing earlier that morning.

"Everything worked perfectly well," he reported. "Just after the Dover post office opened, a man came in and asked for any letters for Roland Frothingham. The clerk handed him an envelope which Frothingham opened. He quickly read the message inside and proceeded to tear the note into pieces and scatter them on the floor."

"Bad luck, that," I said.

Hopkins held up a finger to indicate there was more to come. "As had been prearranged," he went on, "the clerk motioned to a uniformed constable standing in the shadows, and the policeman moved forward. Frothingham was immediately apprehended—not arrested, mind—and urged by the local constabulary to come back here to Scotland Yard. At first, he refused, but when he considered the opportunity to clear his name—not to mention the threat of being hunted down on the Continent—well, he chose to come."

"Excellent," said Holmes.

"I wonder what the note said," I mused.

"Not to worry, Doctor," smiled Hopkins. "The alert constable gathered up the bits of paper and put them into an envelope. Frothingham, along with the envelope and the constable himself, arrived on the morning train not an hour ago. When I received the paper fragments, I arranged them in proper order. It took but a matter of minutes, and I used some mucilage to secure the reconstructed note to a blank page. I have it right here in my coat." Hopkins tapped his breast pocket for emphasis."

In response, Holmes moved his coffee cup to the side and pointed to the space on the table directly in front of him.

Hopkins produced the puzzle-like paper, set it where Holmes had indicated, and the three of us read the message sent to Roland Frothingham:

My uncle has been killed. Following the unfortunate incident at the party, it's best you complete the plan we discussed and leave the country. Let us put off for now any talk of marriage.

[It was signed] *Olivia*

"Most enlightening," observed Sherlock Holmes.

"Ah," smiled Hopkins proudly, "but there is more to tell, Mr. Holmes. The St. John's Wood Road station is just a few minutes' walk from here, and assuming that Frothingham would have begun his journey to Dover as quickly as possible—"

"A *probable* assumption," interrupted Holmes, "but an assumption none the less."

"In any case," the inspector continued, "I went straight to the booking office and found the station-master. A short, moustachioed fellow with a discerning look, he figured right away that I was investigating the murder of Clive Watney-Banks. I can tell you he was quite willing to talk."

"Good thinking, Hopkins. What did you learn there?" asked Holmes.

"Well, he said it was an interesting night compared to the usually quiet Sunday evenings he faces. He spoke in particular about two curious fares. When I presented Frothingham's description, he said that was one of them. He remembered Frothingham because he asked about the quickest place to get a train to Dover. Not a usual question here in St. John's Wood. The station-master told him to get to Victoria and go from there."

"My advice, exactly," I said.

"And yet," continued Hopkins, "we lack any proof that Frothingham actually went to Dover late

61

Sunday night. Oh, it's obvious that he got there eventually. He stayed in a pension on Monday night, but what we don't know is the circuitous route he may have originally taken, where he might have stopped along the way, and what mischief he might have performed there. In a word, gentlemen, we have no evidence directly tying Frothingham to the murder."

"The shot he took at Watney-Banks the day before," I offered.

"Indeed," said Hopkins, "that and his apparent plan to escape via Dover make him our premier suspect."

"Good work, Inspector," I said. "You've made real progress."

"What about the second traveller you mentioned?" Holmes asked.

"A stranger who arrived earlier that same night," Hopkins said. "About half-eight. There were very few passengers coming through, and the station-master knows all of the locals. So here comes a bewhiskered fellow in a dark ulster and slouch hat fresh off the down-train. He'd come into the station with no luggage and asked the station-master the way to Woodlawn House. Then he asked how late the trains ran."

"Interesting," said Holmes leaning forward, eyes ablaze. "Tell me more."

"Well, the same fellow came back a few hours later—maybe ten-thirty or eleven—not long after Frothingham had come by. The slouch hat and ulster were the same, but there were also differences. This time he was carrying a leather grip. What's more, the station-master expected him to take the up-train back towards the city from where he'd come, but he bought a ticket to West Hampstead instead. Not that there's anything amiss with such behaviour, mind, but being a stranger, he drew the station-master's attention."

"Curiouser and curiouser," murmured Holmes.

Hopkins took a final sip of his coffee before informing us that his afternoon would be devoted to setting up the next day's inquest—a jury needed to be formed and the venue confirmed. What is more, for the benefit of the coroner in charge of the formalities, he had to compose a report that presented the salient features of the murder and the subsequent investigation.

At least for the present, Sherlock Holmes and I would continue our stay at Woodlawn House. For Holmes in particular, both its anonymity and distance from central London seemed sources of comfort. For my part, during what remained of the afternoon, not only did I plan to look in on my surgery, but I also needed to post my letter to Dr. Ottolengui.

Chapter Five

The Inquest
(Part I)

[Fiction should be]
something a little different from
the realm of daily experience.
                    --Rodrigues Ottolengui
                    "Preface"
                    The Crime of the Century

*T*he inquest took place on a cold and gloomy Wednesday morning in the St. John's Wood police station, a mid-century, yellow-brick three-storey in Newcourt Street. Framed in white, a single black door served as the entrance. The station, along with its cells for wrong-doers and living quarters for the district's policemen, contained a magistrate courtroom large enough to encompass the proceedings concerning the death of Clive Watney-Banks.

By the time Sherlock Holmes and I arrived, large groups of people had already gathered on the sidewalk.

"Probably safer to be in a crowd," Holmes said loudly enough for me to hear. Even so, he passed cautiously through the group, looking about to see if he recognised anyone who might pose a threat. Observing none, he moved forward.

As is the case with most such public proceedings, the milling throng knew just enough facts to allow pontification by rumour, the so-called pipe upon which played—at least, according to Shakespeare—the "discordant wavering multitude."

"Watney-Banks," someone claimed, "was murdered during a robbery."

"Yet nothing was taken, was it?" countered someone else.

"'Twas the dead man's son what killed him," purported another. "To gain the inheritance."

"But the will don't leave him nothing," a self-styled expert pointed out.

"Didn't know that, did he?" came the reply.

On and on it went:

"What about that footman Watney-Banks sacked last year. . .?"

"Or the greasy beggar who come looking for trouble. . .?"

Paying no attention to such ill-founded claims, Holmes and I weaved our way through the voluble crowd and into the courtroom, a large chamber panelled in dark wood with brass fixtures and wrought-iron railings. A number of people had managed to obtain seats, but the recognizable members of the *dramatis personae* related to the Watney-Banks murder case were not among them.

The relevant witnesses had been sequestered together in a private chamber so they would not be affected by hearing what others before them had to say under oath. Charles Watney-Banks, the newly arrived son, served as the exception. He was seated near the front of the room in the centre of a number of empty chairs, spaces reserved for the others after they had completed their testimonies.

As for Roland Frothingham, he had been kept entirely separate. The Dover police had brought him back to Scotland Yard the day before, and he had been detained until Hopkins had brought him to the St. John's Wood police station early that morning. In order to prevent any of the other witnesses from learning of Frothingham's presence, the inspector had immediately isolated him in an upstairs room. Clearly, Hopkins wanted the appearance of the chief suspect to be a surprise.

Dr. Nathaniel Clifton, the coroner in charge of the proceedings, was an elderly gentleman with piercing dark eyes and a shock of white hair that frequently tumbled over his forehead. I knew the fellow by reputation, a fair man who had experience as both a medical doctor and a criminal lawyer. It was to him that Stanley Hopkins handed a file, presumably the report Hopkins had written the night before.

The coroner's jury—seven local men who were fulfilling their civic responsibility—took their seats on a bench in the jury box to the right of the witness chair. Each member stood, gave his name, and sat down again—each member swearing agreement (if at all possible) to reach a verdict determining cause of death and who or what might have been responsible.

The enquiry began with Inspector Hopkins' repeating to the jury the facts that he (along with the unnamed Sherlock Holmes) had garnered in connection with the crime and the pursuant investigation. How Clive Watney-Banks had been shot twice and killed. How the deceased had fallen into the fire. How the blood on the library floor had been discovered along with the bullet hole in the window and another in the ceiling containing a .44 calibre projectile. How the wedding ring that remained on the man's finger precluded the idea of robbery. How, from scrutiny of the varying depths and sizes of the footprints in the snow surrounding Woodlawn House, one could determine much about the human activity in the area before and after half past nine in the evening, the time the snow was reported to have stopped falling and one-half hour before it was speculated that the murder took place.

Even though I was the first physician to examine the body, Dr. Clifton called upon the medical examiner, Mr. Roger Gabriel, to describe the crime to the coroner's jury. It was the grey-bearded Dr. Gabriel, after all, who had performed the autopsy. Furthermore, the doctor possessed a broad knowledge of forensic medicine and ably reconstructed what was known of the murder.

"Clive Watney-Banks died some time before midnight on Sunday," Gabriel said. "Due to the fire into which Mr. Watney-Banks had fallen, his face was burnt beyond recognition. There were no identifiable markings on his body. Still, the wedding ring and the nightdress with his monogram on the pocket—*CWB*—established the identity of the corpse. His niece, Olivia Watney-Banks, confirmed as much."

Asked to describe the two wounds, Gabriel said, "Both bullets entered from the left side—one shot passed through the body doing little damage; the other, just next to it, hit Watney-Banks directly in the heart and killed him instantly. Powder burns on the victim's night dress indicated that the fatal bullet had been fired at close range. I extracted that bullet, a .44 calibre; I have it right here."

Dr. Gabriel reached into his pocket and produced an envelope. From it, he withdrew the lead projectile and held it between his thumb and forefinger. "Strange to say," he admitted, "the other bullet, the less damaging one, has yet to be found."

"Given the angle of the wounds," Dr. Clifton asked, "do you believe the shots could have come from outside the window?"

"Yes, possibly, depending on how near to the window and in what position Mr. Watney-Banks was standing."

Olivia was called next. Clothed in black, she slowly approached the witness box, her blond hair spun into a tight *chignon*. Clifton asked her to verify not only that it was she who had discovered the body (though she said she had heard no shots fired), but also as a first-hand witness to confirm that Roland Frothingham had attempted to fire his pistol in a moment of anger at her deceased uncle just a few hours before her uncle's actual murder. However reluctantly she agreed to the latter point, throughout her testimony she remained very much in control of her feelings and sentiments and maintained her composure as, after being dismissed, she took her place in a front-row seat.

To clear them of suspicion, Dr. Clifton next called the temporary employees at Woodlawn House— the footman (whom I recognised from the garden party); a gardener; and the stable master—all servants who were available for employment when needed, but who also worked at other houses in the general vicinity. They lived in a small boarding house down the road from Woodlawn, and all of them had spent the time of the murder on Sunday night at the Duke of York, the same pub where Holmes and I had met with Hopkins two nights before. Yes, they all agreed, any number of witnesses including the publican, would verify their whereabouts.

Clifton called David Belford next.

Belford confirmed the story of the shooting at the garden *fêst*, but he maintained that the shot had been accidental and not intended to harm anyone. "I think Rollo's pistol went off when his arm was hit by Olivia," he said. "Otherwise, he never would have fired it."

"Let me be clear, Mr. Belford," said Dr. Clifton. "By 'Rollo,' you are referring to Mr. Roland Frothingham, a person for whom you possess a great feeling of indebtedness."

"Yes. Correct on both points."

"And the basis for your indebtedness?"

"Three years ago, I was walking alongside the Regent's Canal, and I tripped and fell in. I hit my head as I went down, and I'm not much of a swimmer anyway. By myself, I would have drowned, but this fellow I didn't even know—that was Rollo—happened to be there and went in after me. He pulled me out and got me breathing again. He saved my life. I owe him everything. We've been friends ever since."

"A touching story, but might not such indebtedness include minimizing your friend's hatred for the deceased?"

"No."

"Are you currently a member of the St. John's Wood Shooters Club?"

"No."

"Have you ever been?"

"No."

"But you do own a pistol."

"Yes."

"Same as theirs?"

"Yes, in fact, I have it with me." To the consternation of those sitting nearby, David Belford reached into his coat pocket and extracted a revolver that, save for lacking a silver mounting, resembled the guns of his friends.

Clifton looked at it and verified that it was the same model Smith and Wesson. "One round has been fired."

"Yes, but not at Clive Watney-Banks. I fired it during the shooting match. Nothing to do with Mr. Watney-Banks. I never saw him after the garden party."

"But after the garden party, did you remain at Woodlawn House—that is, the night of the murder?"

"Yes."

"Just what was your business there at night, Mr. Belford?"

The poor fellow's face turned red. "I'd rather not say."

As Belford was not compelled to furnish an explanation at the inquest, Clifton excused him, and Belford seated himself in one of the chairs facing the front.

His lady-friend, Rose Greener, the house-keeper at Woodlawn, came next. Today she was dressed in a white shirtwaist and dark-blue walking skirt beneath a long wool coat of navy-blue.

Though David Belford was no longer the witness, after establishing that Rose Greener too was not a member of the shooters club, Dr. Clifton focused on Belford in questioning her. "On the subject of Mr. Belford's loyalty to Roland Frothingham, do you think he might go so far as taking the blame for the murder himself if charges happen to be filed against his friend?"

"Yes, but I know that David didn't do this terrible murder."

"How can you be so certain?"

She looked at Belford, now sitting before her, his florid colour returning. But he nodded acquiescence.

"We were alone together in the greenhouse, you see."

Murmurs and not a few gasps escaped from the audience.

The woman sat up straight, and she stared down those who had sounded offended. "Oh, you don't need to be so shocked," she said, her voice full of defiance. "David and I are going to be married. And he left about 8:30—well before the time poor Mr. Watney-Banks was shot."

"You're certain it was that early?"

"Oh, yes. Though the gas lamps in the lanes had been lit for some time, I still had duties to perform before I left for my digs, didn't I?—turning down beds, restoring the fires, and the like. I remember that it was still snowing, and David—well, he wanted to stay longer, of course."

A few dry chuckles evoked a menacing look from Dr. Clifton, and following a pregnant silence, he continued his questions.

"Mr. Belford could have returned later—without your knowledge, could he not?" Clifton asked.

"I suppose he could, but I know he didn't. He had no reason, you see, not after I left."

Clifton smiled, no doubt at the *naïveté* of the woman's answer. "But before you left, did you hear or see anything of a suspicious nature?"

"More than an hour later, I discovered that I had misplaced my key, and I returned to the greenhouse to look for it. The greenhouse is by a sidewall of the main house, and I didn't see anything strange. It was some time near ten o'clock. That was when I heard two quick gunshots—maybe even a third, I can't be sure."

"And did you find it?"

"Find what?"

"Your key?"

"Oh, yes."

Reggie Folger came next.

Although Clifton knew the answer in advance, for the sake of the jury he began by asking, "Are you currently a member of a society called the St. John's Wood Shooters Club?"

"Yeh, guilty," Reggie Folger answered with a smile, "but I wouldn't call it a society. There are just the four of us."

Like David Belford, Reggie too defended Roland Frothingham. Reggie too had witnessed the gunshot gone awry at the birthday celebration, and like Belford, Reggie too claimed that Roland had no intention of actually harming Olivia's uncle. "The gun went off when Livy hit Rollo's arm. It was an accident. Her uncle was like a father to Livy. Why would Rollo want to do such a terrible thing?"

"How did *you* feel towards Clive Watney-Banks?"

"I didn't like the man. He had no good reason to prevent Rollo from marrying Livy."

"Did you express those feelings to him?"

"Yeh, I might have. Don't remember for sure. Maybe I just imagined the satisfaction I'd feel if I'd actually threatened him myself."

"Were you at Woodlawn House Sunday night? We have footprints suggesting you were at the summer-house."

"Yeh, I met Livy there. She'd sent me a note."

"Do you still have the note?"

"No, sorry. I must have lost it. It said that she wanted to see me. She's a friend, so I went. And when our meeting ended, she left. I think she headed for the canal. But if you want to know what we talked about, you'll have to ask her because I'm no snitch."

"We have reason to believe that after your meeting in the summer-house, you were attacked by the Watney-Banks dog—bitten, in fact."

In reply, Folger held up a bandaged wrist heretofore concealed by his coat-sleeve. "I got quite the fright. That Hengist is a beast. To be honest, after he sprang at me, I don't remember much that happened."

Dr. Clifton produced the gun with Reggie Folger's name on the handle. "Is this your pistol?"

"Yeh."

"It was found Monday morning in the snow on the grounds of Woodlawn House. But, you see, there was no snow covering it, so it could only have been dropped *after* the snowfall ended about half nine—*any* time after half past nine. Which means you could have had it at the time of the murder."

"Yeh, well, I don't remember losing it. I suppose I dropped it when the dog attacked me."

"One of its bullets has been fired."

Reggie furrowed his brow and looked heavenward. He appeared to be thinking. "Oh, yeh, I remember now. I did shoot at the dog, but I missed, you see. That's when I ran off. So did the dog—frightened by the gunshot. Some watchdog."

Another bit of laughter rippled through the audience.

"Could it be that contrary to your account, it was your gunshot that actually attracted the dog?"

"What makes you ask such a question? What in the world might I have been shooting at?"

"Mr. Clive Watney-Banks."

Reggie answered the question with a question of his own. "If I wasn't shooting at the dog," he asked with a smirk, "then why would it have run off?"

More laughter.

"Could the bullet you shot at the dog have gone through the window of the house?"

"I suppose so."

"And could it have struck Mr. Watney-Banks?"

"No! I mean, I suppose it could have. But look—the dog ran one way; I ran the other. I might have heard another shot, maybe two. But I can't be certain."

Dr. Clifton next called Eugenia Frothingham. As soon as she entered the courtroom, she looked round for her friends and smiled nervously when she recognised them in the front-section seats.

Clifton began with the predictable question. "Are you now a member of a society called the St. John's Wood Shooters Club?"

"Yes," she replied softly.

"Speak up, please."

"Yes!"

"When did you learn of Clive Watney-Banks' death?"

"Monday morning. Olivia came to our house. She told me the news about her uncle's murder."

"And this came as a surprise to you?"

"I don't know," Eugenia said sheepishly. "Somehow, it seems I already knew. Or guessed it. Or dreamed it. I was there that night, you see—at Woodlawn. The night of the murder. I was hiding in the summer-house. I decided to go there because I had suspicions."

"What sort of suspicions?"

"Reggie told me he was going out of town Sunday afternoon, but then I found a note he dropped. I recognised Livy's handwriting and—well, I admit that I am the jealous-type, so I read it. The note said Olivia wanted to meet with him. He had lied to me about going away. Livy's my friend and is close to my brother,

Roland, but I wanted to know why she asked to meet with my Reggie. And I took along my pistol. I don't even know why." As she spoke, her eyes began to glisten.

Just as Holmes had pictured, Eugenia reported how she had hidden behind a wall in the summer-house and listened to the conversation between her suitor and her friend. "I know now," she said with a sob, "that I was foolish to mistrust Reggie."

Eugenia dabbed at her eyes with a lace handkerchief, and Dr. Clifton waited a moment before asking her what she had overheard in the summer-house.

"Livy told Reggie that Rollo had asked her to marry him—that Rollo had told her that agreeing to marry him was the only way he would stay here. If she said no, he would take the train to Dover, cross to the Continent on the Dover-Calais packet, and exit Livy's life forever."

Bold plans, I thought—so bold, in fact, that according to Eugenia, after Olivia told Roland she still would not marry him without her uncle's consent, Olivia began to worry that rather than crossing the Channel, Roland would do something foolhardy.

"Like kill her uncle?" Dr. Clifton asked.

"Like kill *himself,*" Eugenia countered. "Livy's uncle was alive when Reggie left Sunday night."

"Did you see the dog attack Reggie?"

"No, I was still behind the wall in the summer-house. I heard the dog barking, and I heard the shot Reggie fired. He missed the dog, and I heard the bullet break the glass in the library window."

"But you didn't actually see anything of the encounter with the dog, so you don't know for certain that Reggie was shooting at the animal and not at the deceased."

"I know he didn't shoot Livy's uncle. I know because after Reggie fired, I looked up and saw Mr. Watney-Banks raise the sash, aim his own pistol and return the shot, then close the window. For certain, he had not been hit. Fortunately for Reggie and me, Mr. Watney-Banks was not a good shot. I think he feared an intruder that had been found out by his dog."

At this point, Eugenia paused in her testimony. She clasped her hands tightly round the handkerchief she was still holding and sat in silence for a long minute. Finally, she said, "The next morning I couldn't find my gun." A moment later, she announced, "I know that Reggie Folger did not shoot Clive Watney-Banks, Dr. Clifton. And neither did my brother or anyone else." As she continued, her voice turned tremulous. "I can say that with certainty because"—here she paused to take a breath—"because *I* am the one who did so. *I* am the person who killed Livy's uncle."

Then the poor woman fainted. Slumping in her chair, she was prevented from slipping to the floor only by the quick action of Dr. Clifton.

Gasps filled the courtroom. Some people stood. Dr. Clifton, who produced smelling salts from his pocket, quickly brought the unfortunate soul back to consciousness. As directed by the doctor, a uniformed policeman escorted the shaken young woman into an adjoining room.

Dr. Clifton raised his hands as he stood before the rest of us in the chamber. "This inquest will be in recess for fifteen minutes," he announced. Then he pushed back the shock of white hair that had fallen across his forehead and followed Eugenia Frothingham and the constable out of the magistrate courtroom.

Chapter Six

The Inquest
(Part II)

We're all honest, till we're caught.
                        --Rodrigues Ottolengui
                        The Phoenix of Crime

During the recess, Sherlock Holmes and I huddled with Hopkins and Clifton to discuss the implications of Eugenia's confession. One might be tempted to think that her admission ended the matter— the murderer had identified herself and the inquest could be brought to an end. But we all agreed that such a conclusion would be precipitous.

The fifteen minutes passed quickly, and the jury was recalled. "Simply put, gentlemen," Dr. Clifton said in front of the jury box, "since one cannot be certain that the bullet in the library's ceiling had not been fired by Eugenia Frothingham's gun, no matter how much she may personally believe her own confession, she cannot be confirmed as the shooter who killed Clive Watney-Banks."

Nor could Reggie Folger be the killer—if Eugenia's account were accurate. She had reported how Watney-Banks—clearly very much alive at the time— had come to the window after hearing the shot Reggie had fired wildly at Hengist the dog and discharged a gun himself in Reggie's general direction. In a word, Eugenia's testimony proved nothing.

"Gentlemen," Dr. Clifton informed the jury, "we must press on. More evidence is required."

Repositioning himself at the front of the chamber, Dr. Clifton cleared his throat and announced he was recalling Olivia Watney-Banks. Once she was seated, Clifton reminded her she remained under oath. Then to no one's surprise he asked, "Are you now a member of a society called the St. John's Wood Shooters Club?"

"Yes," she answered. "I organised the club myself."

(It was during this second testimony that Olivia explained the history that I reported earlier detailing her fascination with guns.)

"Please describe what happened at Woodlawn House on Sunday night," Dr. Clifton said.

"Late Sunday evening I went out to meet two of my friends—first, Reggie Folger in the summer-house and then Roland Frothingham by the canal. Being out at night, I originally planned to bring my pistol, but I changed my mind and left it on the mantel in the library."

"If you left your pistol on the mantel, how did it end up in your room Monday morning when Inspector Hopkins arrived?"

"Sunday night, besides my uncle, I was the only person in the house at the time of his murder—excluding the killer, of course. I heard no shots. But when I discovered my uncle's body early the next morning, I also saw my gun on the floor. I'm not stupid. The gun has my name on it. I thought someone might have used it to shoot my uncle and blame it on me. So I picked it up and took it to my room to avoid being implicated in the crime myself."

"Recall the wire brush next to the wash basin," Holmes whispered to me. "Not only did the woman reclaim her pistol, she cleaned and reloaded it as well."

"What about the empty casing you found on the floor?" I whispered back.

"After she reloaded the gun, she must have realised that she should have left the empty casing in the cylinder where it had been following her final shot in the shooting match. To avoid the appearance of trying to conceal the use of her pistol, she replaced a fresh bullet in the gun with another empty shell like the one on the floor."

"Ingenious," I murmured.

Meanwhile, Olivia's narrative moved from her actions in the house to her meetings with some of the principals in the case. "Having told Rollo previously that I would not elope with him, I decided to meet with his friend Reggie. I wanted to ask Reggie to look out for Rollo, to make sure Rollo would be all right. I had just rejected him, you see, and one never knows how a man will react in such a situation. In light of his anger earlier that afternoon, I feared he might do something extreme—"

"Like kill your uncle who forbade your marriage?" interrupted Dr. Clifton. It was the same question he had put to Eugenia Frothingham previously.

"No," Olivia replied just as her friend had done. "Like kill *himself*."

Dr. Clifton now directed Olivia to relate what happened following her meeting with Reggie Folger.

"I walked to the Regent's Canal where I met with Rollo. Once again, I told him that I would not run off with him. It would be too devastating for my uncle. This time, I felt the message had got through. After our meeting, I walked back to Woodlawn."

"When did you return?"

"About ten-thirty. Well after the time people said they heard gunshots."

"And Roland? What did he do?"

"I assumed that he'd gone off on his own."

"To where?"

"As I told Inspector Hopkins, Rollo usually stays in a cottage his family owns in West Hampstead. They don't use it often."

"In West Hampstead, you say. Where is this cottage specifically?"

"I believe it's near Fortune Green Lane—just east of West End Lane."

"Really!" said Clifton, eyebrows arched. "You're most precise." No sooner did he complete his praise, however, than he returned to his file on the front table and produced the reconstituted message that Olivia had sent to Dover, the note for Roland that said he should leave the country.

"I suggest to you, Miss Watney-Banks, that you knew that Roland Frothingham was nowhere near West Hampstead late Sunday night—I suggest that you knew exactly where he was—on his way to Dover where he would be waiting to hear from you."

Olivia covered her eyes with her hands. When she returned them to her lap, she said simply, "He's innocent. Because of the trouble earlier in the day, I thought it would be safer for him if he left."

"So you yourself lied just now to protect him."

"Yes."

"Did you know that Roland Frothingham had returned to Woodlawn House after your meeting?"

Olivia paused before answering.

"No," she said at last.

"Would you like to know why?"

"Very much."

"I'll tell you what, Miss Watney-Banks," proclaimed Dr. Clifton with a dramatic sweep of his arm, "why don't I ask Roland himself that very question?"

A look of alarm crossed Olivia's face, her expression of shock fulfilling Hopkins' hoped-for surprise. Nor was the startled look confined to Olivia. No sooner had Dr. Clifton announced, "I call Roland Frothingham as a witness," than all heads turned in astonishment to see the so-named fugitive emerge from a door at the side of the courtroom.

At the same time Olivia Watney-Banks was returning to her seat, her ill-fated suitor was slowly making his way to the witness chair. Standing in white shirt, dark waistcoat, and dark trousers, he took the oath, but before sitting down, looked briefly at Olivia. He displayed for her what appeared to be a reassuring smile and then turned to face his questioner.

"You don't live in St. John's Wood, do you, Mr. Frothingham," Clifton began.

"No."

"Where, in fact, do you live?"

"My family has a vacation cottage in West Hampstead."

Holmes leaned over to me. "Not an answer to the question," he whispered.

By now, the next query was predictable: "Are you presently a member of a society called the St. John's Wood Shooters Club?"

"Yes."

"Why did you return to Woodlawn House following your Sunday-night meeting with Olivia Watney-Banks by the canal?"

If Roland experienced surprise at Clifton's knowledge of the clandestine meeting, the young man did not reveal it.

"I went back to the house because I felt the meeting went wrong. At the canal, I had intended to ask Livy one last time to marry me—without the approval of her uncle. When she refused and left, I felt so disappointed that I decided I'd try one last time to convince her uncle to drop his objection."

"Did Olivia know of your plan?"

"I wanted to tell her before I spoke to her uncle. It may sound silly, but as I passed by the side of the house, I actually rehearsed the plea for support I was planning to make to her."

"Did you go inside?"

"Don't you know? You seem to know everything else."

"Unfortunately, Mr. Frothingham, there was no snow inside the house to reveal your footprints. I ask again, did you go inside?"

"I suppose I should say that I saw Clive Watney-Banks alive and well through the library window."

"Only if that is true."

"If I say that I did, you will accuse me of murder. If I say that I did not, that I looked through the library window and saw nothing amiss, you may say I am lying. In any case, I could see from the outside of the house that Livy's light was out, and I did not wish to disturb her. So I left . . . without going in."

The young man's resolve was impressive. He and Olivia made a strong pair.

But Dr. Clifton was not yet finished with Roland Frothingham. Next to Clifton's file on the front table stood a small wooden box, which he proceeded to open.

From inside it, he withdrew the gold locket that Holmes had found in the dead man's hand. Holding it up in front of Frothingham's face, Clifton popped open the tiny case. "A thumb-nail portrait of the young Olivia Watney-Banks inside," he proclaimed to the members of the jury. "Engraved *JF to AF* on the outside."

"Impossible," whispered the young man, his eyes opening wide, his hands patting his own pockets as if to feel their contents. "Wh—where did you find that?"

"What do you know about it?"

Frothingham hung his head. "I—I stole it from Olivia."

"Oh, Rollo," Olivia cried out.

"That was weeks ago," he said, "when I feared I had no chance with her. It was a keepsake. Foolish, I know. I carry it—I mean, I carried it—with me all the time. I realise now I must have lost it somewhere. How did you come to possess it?"

By admitting that he had taken the locket from Olivia, the locket which had been found in the grip of the dead man, Roland Frothingham had clearly incriminated himself. He had admitted to motive and opportunity, and we had already heard that Olivia had left her pistol on the mantel in the room in which Frothingham had confronted her uncle. The locket now placed Roland himself at the scene of the murder. Such thoughts could only lead—

"Enough!" The defiant voice of Olivia Watney-Banks interrupted my thoughts. "Leave him alone. I am the one. I shot my uncle."

Young Frothingham looked startled. Then he shook his head.

Throughout the courtroom silence reigned. Another confession. First, Eugenia; now, Olivia.

It took a few moments for Dr. Clifton to collect himself. When he did, he managed to tell Frothingham to find a seat and to order Olivia to the witness chair for the third time.

Olivia stood, looked back at her cousin, Charles, for support, then walked determinedly to the witness chair.

The moment she was seated, Clifton said, "Again, I ask you to describe what happened the night Clive Watney-Banks died. Only this time, I expect you to tell us the truth. I remind you once more that you are still under oath."

Olivia took a deep breath and then spoke slowly. "After returning from my meeting with Rollo, I wanted to be honest with my uncle. I saw that he was in the library, and so I confronted him there. I told him I had been with Rollo earlier, and before I could say anything else, my uncle became very angry. He was outraged that I should maintain any kind of relationship with a Frothingham—with *any* Frothingham. His point of view was intolerable, and fearing for my safety, I remembered that I had left my gun on the mantel. I retrieved it and shot him."

"How many times?"

"Once."

"But he was shot twice."

A furrow crossed her brow. This moment seemed to present to her for the first time the nature of her uncle's wounds. One must remember that Olivia had not been in the courtroom for Hopkins' initial summary of the crime or for Medical Examiner Gabriel's description of the two wounds. For their part, neither Holmes nor Hopkins had told her either.

Olivia paused a moment as if to collect her thoughts. "Oh, I remember now. My uncle—he—he told me he was struck by Rollo's bullet in the afternoon, but it was nothing serious."

"Rollo's bullet, was it?" Clifton said, disbelief evident in his mimicry.

"I have nothing more to say."

Charles smiled at her, presumably in appreciation of her strength—though, singularly enough, her strength in admitting to the murder of his father.

Taken all together, it was a strange inquest. Of the four members of the Shooters Club, two—the young women—had confessed to killing the same man; another, Folger, also admitted to firing his pistol; and the fourth, Roland Frothingham, could be placed at the scene of the crime.

Yet the culpability of both Eugenia and Folger was open to question; there was no proof that either of their bullets had found Clive Watney-Banks' heart. In terms of actually firing a pistol that Sunday night, there was even less evidence concerning Frothingham. Olivia's admission, on the other hand, was precise.

Dr. Clifton spent the next few minutes advising the coroner's jury on their responsibilities. Afterwards, the seven men retired to a nearby room.

"What do you make of it?" I asked Holmes.

"I don't like it," he said, ticking off on his long fingers each of his concerns: "First, it seems most fortuitous that Miss Watney-Banks chose to confess only when Frothingham's testimony had placed him in the greatest jeopardy."

"Most fortuitous," I agreed.

"Second, we still don't know how Clive Watney-Banks got hold of that locket. Roland seemed as surprised as anyone to discover that it had turned up in the dead man's hand. Third, Olivia produced new information. We have never before heard that Watney-Banks had actually been struck by Roland's bullet at the afternoon party. No one else has presented that detail, and frankly I doubt its veracity. I feel certain that she made it up when she learned that her uncle had been shot twice."

"Anything else?"

"Yes, there's the question about her pistol. Even though Miss Watney-Banks cleaned it, we suspect from the single spent-casing I found on the floor that only one bullet had been fired from her gun. If the single shot was at her uncle, how is it that Eugenia Frothingham could report that Watney-Banks had shot at Reggie with that same pistol? One of the St. John's Wood Shooters is clearly lying—perhaps, all of them are. But wait," Holmes nodded towards a side door. "The jury is returning."

There is no need to draw out the drama. The side door opened, and the jurors quickly returned to their seats. It had taken the seven men less than an hour of deliberation. None of them looked at Olivia—clearly a bad sign for the young lady.

Upon being asked by Dr. Clifton if they had reached a verdict, the foreman rose, ran a hand through his dark hair, and said that they had. "We find the death of Clive Watney-Banks to have been caused by homicide," announced the foreman. "And thanks to her confession, we find Miss Olivia Watney-Banks responsible for his murder."

Chapter Seven

The Aftermath

A properly constructed detective story,
free from pruriency,
is wholesome reading.
--Rodrigues Ottolengui
"Writing Detective Stories"
Quoted by Leslie S. Klinger
"Introduction"
Ottolengui's *Final Proof*

With her head held high and her eyes focused straight ahead, Olivia Watney-Banks was escorted out of the courtroom by a uniformed constable. She would be charged with murder; a trial would follow, and one could only shudder at the prospect of what might transpire if the young woman were found guilty. On a lesser note, one wondered if the poor girl would be allowed to attend her uncle's funeral on Friday, a service that presumably her cousin Charles would now be responsible for arranging.

At the same time the door was closing behind Olivia Watney-Banks, Hopkins approached my friend. "Confession or not, Mr. Holmes," said the inspector shaking his head, "I'm not convinced. There are some facts that don't add up."

"Agreed," said Holmes as we fell in line with the others leaving the building. A few paces in front of us, David Belford and Rose Greener were following Roland Frothingham out the door.

Beneath a threatening sky, Holmes said to the inspector, "In the name of justice, we must continue our investigation."

With a nod, Hopkins signalled for the police van that would take him back to Scotland Yard. Holmes and I, however, decided to risk the rain and walk the short distance to Woodlawn House.

As was now his wont, Holmes turned round to be sure no one was following. He noted nothing of concern, and yet minutes later I heard running footfalls behind us.

"Holmes," I exclaimed, "someone's coming."

"Oh," said he without even a glance over his shoulder, "that's Cousin Charles. Nothing to be alarmed about. He picked up our trail just past the first turning."

A minute passed, and then we were overtaken by Charles Watney-Banks. Since he had no lasting relationship with his cousin Olivia, I assumed that he must be feeling some sort of relief now that he had heard her confession regarding the murder of his father. Yet no sooner did I express that sentiment than he surprised me.

"I think Olivia's innocent," he said. Then he turned to my friend. "What do you make of the verdict, Mr. Holmes?"

"Whilst it is true," Holmes replied, "that British juries do indeed make mistakes, yet Miss Watney-Banks has confessed."

"*If* you believe her," said the cousin.

"Pray," asked Holmes, "why should one *not* believe her?"

It may have sounded to Charles Watney-Banks that his cousin's confession had convinced Holmes of her guilt, yet I knew my friend well enough to recognise that his ambiguous response suggested the opposite. For

Holmes, ambiguity elicited opinions from others, opinions that frequently opened new paths of enquiry.

Quite firm in his own view, Charles Watney-Banks might be one to offer just such a path. "As the dead man was my father," he said, "I paid special attention at the inquest. From all that I heard, I think Olivia confessed in order to give the true murderer the time to escape."

"The true murderer," I repeated. "Who do you reckon that is?"

Watney-Banks put up both his hands in a defensive posture. "I've only been here a short while, gentlemen," said he, "but I definitely feel that my cousin is shielding—what is the name of her so-called paramour? I forget."

"Roland Frothingham," I reminded him.

"Right. One can only assume that she has pleaded guilty in order to allow this Frothingham bloke the opportunity to escape."

"And if he succeeds?" I asked.

"When she believes he has had enough time to reach some distant place, you'll see—she shall recant her plea and probably go off to meet him there. She'll tell the authorities that she was so upset by her uncle's death that she didn't know what she was saying when she confessed. It seems to me that in spite of her cold demeanour, she's quite the sympathetic soul. She could convince most anyone that she had made a mistake. She certainly has convinced *me*."

One could not find fault with Charles' assessment of the young woman's persuasive talents. What is more, given that we had never shared with her the existence of the double injury, like Holmes, I too wondered at her impromptu explanation of the second wound—chronologically, the first. The suggestion that her uncle had been struck by Roland's bullet after the shooting match did not ring true.

I confess to feeling a degree of sympathy for Olivia Watney-Banks, and yet I did not need Sherlock Holmes to remind me that such sentiment did not necessarily equate with a belief in her innocence. I needed to know more.

"Why are you so convinced that Frothingham is the true killer?" I asked Charles Watney-Banks.

"Look," he replied, "Olivia refused to marry without my father's—that is, her uncle's—permission. His refusal that night was nothing new. Why would she kill her uncle because he continued his traditional protest? No, it was the locket, man. Don't you see? Frothingham admitted to having it, and it wound up in my father's hand. Father could only have grabbed it from him at the scene of the murder. The locket places Frothingham right there when my father was shot."

"He maintains that he never entered the house that night," I said.

Charles shook his head. "A lie. What else to expect from the man who murdered my father?"

Sherlock Holmes remained silent during this discussion. It was clear that he had something in mind, but I could not imagine what it was.

"You have no doubts at all?" I persisted.

"Oh, I do have a question or two," said Charles. "I do wonder what happened to Roland's gun; it must be the murder weapon. I wonder if Olivia knows where it is. Apparently, my father picked it up from the lawn after Frothingham had shot at him during the garden party. My father might have locked it in his desk in the library and taken it out when Frothingham confronted him later that night. Or maybe Father had reached for it when he heard the dog barking so madly and then shot at the intruder who turned out to be this Folger chap. After firing out the window, Father may have put the gun down on the desk where it was available to Frothingham when he came into the room. But look, I don't have any idea what actually happened to it."

"Perhaps," I suggested, "the young man may simply have tossed it into the Regent's Canal once he left Woodlawn House."

"Yet it had his name on it," said Charles. "He wouldn't have wanted to risk its being found. The police might dredge the canal. No, I shouldn't imagine he threw it there. Perhaps, he simply took the gun home with him before he left for Dover. Olivia said he stays at the family cottage in West Hampstead."

"Fortune Green Lane," Holmes reminded us. "That's in the farmland east of West End Lane, the main road. The area on the other side is being converted into housing estates."

"West Hampstead's just a few stations up the train line from here," I pointed out.

"Well," Charles said, "that cottage is certainly where I would start looking."

There was a glint in Holmes' steel-grey eyes. "Watson," he said, "you and I should pay the Frothingham cottage a visit tomorrow morning."

Following a simple breakfast of eggs, toast, and coffee prepared by Rose Greener, Holmes and I walked to the station in Saint John's Wood Road, part of the Metropolitan and St. John's Wood Railway. The train-station itself is a small single-storey of yellow brick at the junction of St. John's Wood Road and Park Road.

Before entering, Holmes checked the roadways to be certain we had not been followed.

When we proceeded into the booking office, the station-master behind the counter got to his feet. With his short stature and black moustache, he was no doubt the same garrulous official spoken to by Hopkins.

"Two tickets to West Hampstead," Holmes said.

The station-master eyed us carefully. "You two are detectives," he smiled. "I can tell. You're here about the murder. The other detective didn't go to West Hampstead, you know."

"Mr. Hopkins?" I asked. "The inspector in the tweed suit?"

"That's the gent. I guess you two must be further along in your investigation than he is."

"Indeed," said Holmes.

A loud whistle alerted us to the arrival of our train, and rather than feed the station-master's appetite for sensational details, Holmes and I hastened to the platform. Belching and hissing like some ponderous animal, the locomotive lumbered to a stop, and Holmes and I entered the first available carriage.

It took but a few minutes to reach the West Hampstead Station. Since we were the only passengers to get off, it was a simple matter to note as we climbed down the stairs that no one was trailing us.

In West End Lane we hired a hansom, and Holmes dared ask the driver if he knew the Frothingham cottage.

"Right you are, guv," the cabbie said, and we immediately headed east. In less than a quarter of an hour, we found ourselves in an isolated patch of land between a pair of buildings—a square, red-brick house identified by the driver as West End Hall and an Italianate edifice of three storeys called Canterbury

House replete with low roof, arched windows, and ornate fixings. The Frothingham house itself was a small, simple structure set among a group of plane trees.

Once the hansom drove off, we slowly approached the front door. No one responded to Holmes' knock, and we assumed the cottage to be empty.

"Note the scratches about the lock," Holmes said. "I daresay it has been picked."

Indeed, a turn of the handle opened the door, and Holmes and I walked in. An initial glance round the sitting room revealed that nothing appeared to have been disturbed.

"Never overlook a fireplace," Holmes said as he crossed over to the hearth and gingerly fingered the ashes. "Cold. No one has been here recently."

"Roland must be staying somewhere else," I offered.

Holmes did not reply. Already sifting through the debris on the grate, he now held up some blackened bits and pieces. "Cloth and the remains of a button—clothing, without a doubt." He fished about some more and, extracting a few pieces of wire, evoked his experiences on the stage. "Something with which I am familiar," he said, "the foundation of a false beard. Note the ear hooks."

Holmes tossed the wire back onto the grate, stood up, and peered about. "I'll look in the bedrooms, Watson; you examine the kitchen."

The kitchen floor consisted of unglazed, ceramic square tiles decorated in hues of red and brown with various geometric shapes—triangles, squares, and the like. It was one of the tiles with a reddish rectangle that revealed the prize. I had barely entered the room when I tripped over its raised edge. Looking at the tile more closely, I saw that it had been badly laid. More to the point, when I lifted the square piece, I discovered a small hidey-hole beneath it.

"Holmes," I called out, surveying my find, "in here." As he entered the kitchen, I slowly pulled out of the cavity a silver-mounted .44 calibre Smith and Wesson Number Three revolver. On its handle, the engraved name of a member of the St. John's Wood Shooting Club was clearly visible: *Roland Frothingham.*

I handed the gun to Holmes, and he examined the chambers. "Fired three times," said he.

"Once, at the birthday party," I offered, "and twice more into Watney-Banks."

Holmes smelt the gun. "Perhaps," he said. Then he surprised me by asking, "How did you discover this?"

"I literally stumbled over the loose tile."

"How loose was it?"

"Extremely loose."

"As if it was meant to be stumbled over," observed Holmes. "Very convenient. Like the unlocked front door. Let us return to Woodlawn."

We looked through the rest of the cottage, but found nothing else of relevance besides the pistol. Holmes pocketed the weapon and after taking the train back to the St. John's Wood Road Station, we returned to Woodlawn House without incident.

Stanley Hopkins was in the sitting room talking to Charles Watney-Banks when we arrived. Holmes interrupted their conversation to hand the inspector the gun and tell him how and where we discovered it.

"You were right," I told Charles. "The place to look was the cottage in West Hampstead."

"A lucky guess," said Charles.

Hopkins grinned as he examined the silver pistol. "With Frothingham's name on it," Hopkins said. "One can't ask for much more."

"Hidden—as you described it," observed Charles, "I should think this gun dooms the fellow."

"I'm not so sure," I countered. "Don't forget that Olivia can substantiate Roland's alibi. She says they were together by the canal at ten o'clock, the time Rose Greener said she heard the gunshots."

"Why, Olivia can destroy your case, Inspector," said Charles.

Hopkins shook his head. "Not if you consider her an accomplice."

Watney-Banks frowned. "I hadn't looked at it that way."

"Oh, yes," replied Hopkins, "an accomplice. This pistol—it was hidden, you say?—convinces me that Frothingham was the actual shooter, and it's only logical to believe she'd lie to save him. Let us not forget her fabricated confession at the inquest. Providing false information about the time of her meeting with Frothingham is just another example of her mendacity."

The more Hopkins stated the case against Olivia, the more distressed grew the expression of her cousin.

"I'll be off to the Yard now," said Hopkins, and rubbing his hands together, added, "I think I can wrap things up fairly quickly now."

"Good for you, Inspector," Charles said as he escorted Hopkins to the outer door. Yet in spite of his encouraging words, I saw no change in Charles' troubled countenance.

"There's more to this case than Hopkins realises," Holmes confided to me as we sat alone in the sitting room. "Blaming it on Roland Frothingham is far too simple a solution."

The result of finding Frothingham's pistol was two-fold. Olivia Watney-Banks was freed, and Roland Frothingham was officially arrested for the murder of her uncle. An additional result also occurred: Olivia Watney-Banks offered to Sherlock Holmes whatever aid she could give.

"I know Rollo is innocent," she told us later that afternoon in the sitting room. "I was with him by the canal when my uncle was shot. I want to help, but first I must plan the final details of tomorrow's funeral. The police returned my uncle's body after the autopsy, and Charles has already arranged for him to be buried at Highgate Cemetery. We shall accompany the coffin there from the house. At the same time, I shall do whatever I can to help you free Roland and find my uncle's true killer. Oh, how I wish I had never laid eyes on those pistols."

It was an impassioned plea, and Holmes, I was happy to see, did not let the young woman down.

"In the name of justice," he told her, "I shall find the person responsible for the murder. Like you, in spite of the pistol with his name on it, I do not believe Mr. Frothingham to be the one. But what, Miss Watney-Banks, makes *you* so certain of his innocence? After all, we found his gun hidden in his family's cottage in West Hampstead."

"Because, Mr. Holmes, I don't believe Rollo ever went back there. He wasn't staying in the cottage this past weekend. He was staying on a canal boat so he could be closer to me."

"A canal boat?" I repeated. I knew of the long, commercial vessels moored along the edges of the Regent's Canal, of course. I also knew that although most of them were used for transporting goods like coal, coke, gas, and even ice, some people actually lived in them.

"Whose boat?" Holmes asked.

"Oh, I don't know. Neither did he. Rollo's a squatter. He'd stay on any boat moored nearby. The one he found this time was called the *Marvel*. It was tied up at the northern edge of Regent's Park—very close to the Blow-up Bridge—at least, it was there Sunday night when I met with Rollo on board."

"The Blow-up Bridge," I repeated. "You mean Macclesfield, the bridge that's been rebuilt?"

"Yes," she said, "that's the one."

Most people familiar with the area knew of the bridge that had been accidentally destroyed in a deadly explosion of gunpowder close to twenty years before. Though rebuilt, the bridge retains its dramatic nickname.[*]

"I take it," Holmes said, "that the police do not know about this boat."

Olivia shook her head. "No. Rollo didn't want to admit to trespassing. He wasn't bothering anyone. Is it important?"

"Miss Watney-Banks," said Holmes, "when it's a question of murder, everything is important."

---

[*]In his book, *Julian Hawthorne: The Life of a Prodigal Son*, Gary Scharnhorst reports that Julian Hawthorne, son of author Nathaniel Hawthorne and a member of the American literati in his own right, was living in St. John's Wood at the time and earned a most welcome $50 from the *New York Tribune* for a story about the explosion in 1874 that killed three crew members and caused great distress among the animals in the nearby London Zoo.

"But what can a canal boat have to do with the locket, Holmes?" I asked. "If Frothingham is innocent, how do you account for the locket's winding up in the hand of the dead man?"

It was Miss Watney-Banks who answered. "Rollo must have come in the house and dropped it when he came looking for me, and my uncle picked it up."

"Yet Roland never admitted to entering the house after your meeting Sunday night," I pointed out.

"Well, maybe Rollo dropped it some other time," she said. "It's the only explanation. Even so, the fact that my uncle had it in his hand doesn't mean that Rollo killed him. It's really that simple."

I am afraid that it was her reasoning itself that was too simple to convince me of Roland's innocence— too simple and too convenient.

Holmes put my thoughts into words. "I'm afraid, Miss Watney-Banks, that even if the locket had been dropped on the floor days before, there is no reason to believe your uncle would have picked it up within seconds of being shot."

The young woman said nothing, but her crestfallen look indicated she understood Holmes' point.

"In any case," Holmes said, "we must attend your uncle's funeral on the morrow. In the meantime, there remains much to be learned." As he rose to his feet, he said, "I have one final question."

"Yes, Mr. Holmes?"

"Could you tell me the name of your uncle's dentist?"

The young woman looked at him with a puzzled expression. So did I.

"Why, I believe it is Dr. Carl Davies in Mortimer Street."

Holmes nodded his thanks. "That's about a mile from Baker Street, old fellow," he said to me. Donning his deerstalker and shrugging into his Inverness, he added, "Tomorrow is the funeral, Watson. Do not be alarmed if you don't see me until then. In the meantime, as little as I want to be seen in the streets, I have some questions that need resolution."

He was out the door before I could ask him if he was having trouble with his teeth.

Chapter Eight

Forensic Dentistry

It would be an unexampled coincidence
to find that two persons had obtained
exactly similar dental services.
Would it not?"
--Rodrigues Ottolengui
The Phoenix of Crime

The critic John Ruskin is said to have originated the literary term, "pathetic fallacy," the idea that people are subject to attributing human emotions to non-human occurrences. Ruskin's phrase came to mind with the arrival of a downpour on the Friday morning of Clive Watney-Banks' funeral. The heavens were weeping.

Or so I thought upon waking. Yet as the clock approached eleven, the time set for our departure to Highgate Cemetery, the deluge had transformed into a thin rain.

Still, there was no sign of Sherlock Holmes. True, he had forewarned me about his not returning to Woodlawn House for the night, and yet I knew he wanted to observe the various individuals during the burial. "The more funereal a ceremony for the dead," he once said to me at graveside, "the more revelatory the exercise for the living."

Fittingly or ironically (I could not decide which), the coffin had been placed in the library, the chamber where the murder of its occupant had taken place. Made of oak, it rested on the seats of four chairs, two pairs facing each other. In deference to the horrible damage done to the dead man's head, the lid remained closed.

A subdued group of mourners all dressed in black had braved the weather to join the procession to the cemetery. I recognised some of them from the inquest and others from the Sunday birthday celebration, which had ended so dramatically.

In particular, I searched for George Hampson, Clive Watney-Banks' museum colleague, but he was nowhere to be seen. By then, of course, I had come to appreciate his comment about Watney-Banks' temper as more of a warning than a mere observation. To think it had been less than a week that I had enquired of Hampson regarding an etymological artist for Dr. Ottolengui, less than a week since that enquiry indirectly led to the gunfire at Olivia's birthday celebration. It felt so much longer.

As mourners stood by, the bearers raised the coffin by its brass handles and, carrying it smoothly, walked slowly out of the library, through the hallway, and out the front door. Continuing along the short path from the outer door to the red-brick gate-posts, the coffin progressed to the waiting hearse and its matched pair of true-black Friesian horses. One of the bearers was already opening the rear door of the carriage in preparation of placing the coffin within, and still there was no sign of Holmes.

Suddenly, the sound of horses' hooves broke the mournful silence, and a police van pulled by two high-stepping, black draught horses careened into view. The wet roadway caused the van to skid, but the skilled driver managed to keep the horses calm and not pull up instantly which would have worsened the slide.

The van came to a halt about fifty feet beyond the hearse, and before it fully stopped, Sherlock Holmes bolted from the door, Inspector Hopkins trailing more sedately behind him.

"Stop!" Holmes shouted. "Take the coffin back in the house."

The bearers looked confused, but Hopkins, assuring them of his authority, repeated Holmes' instruction, and the coffin was slowly, if with less dignity, returned to the quartet of chairs upon which it had rested.

Together the two cousins came rushing up to Holmes. "What is happening?" an upset Olivia Watney-Banks questioned, her blond hair looking almost white in contrast to her black frock.

"You can't do this to my father," said Charles, his face almost as rubicund as his hair. "The poor man's been through enough already."

Holmes produced a screwdriver with which he began the task of freeing the lid of the coffin. Olivia moved to stop him, but Hopkins held her back.

"This is most urgent," the inspector explained.

"It is most disturbing," she replied.

"Inspector," Charles pleaded.

"Sorry," Hopkins murmured as he ushered both Olivia and Charles out of the library and closed the door.

For the next few minutes, the inspector and I watched Holmes proceed with his macabre task. At last, the lid fell away.

"Good," said Holmes as he motioned us to his side. "The corpse still wears the wedding ring."

I for one moved forward with some trepidation though I don't know why I felt so uncomfortable. I am a doctor, after all, who has served during wartime and seen the most unspeakable results of man's ability to wreak havoc on the human anatomy. Besides, when I first examined the body, I had already witnessed the frightening remains of Clive Watney-Banks' horribly disfigured features. Nonetheless, I was relieved to discover that the charred head had been swathed in white silk. Judging from the breath Hopkins let out, he must have felt the same.

"Note the position of the ring," Holmes whispered, nodding in the direction of the dead man's hands, which were crossed upon his breast. It was the same ring to which he referred that, along with the monogram on the night-dress, had helped the police identify the body as that of Watney-Banks. The ring rested just beyond the first knuckle of the fourth finger of the left hand.

"Shouldn't it be pushed past the second knuckle?" I asked quietly. "The ring appears in danger of falling off."

"It won't move," Holmes surprised me by saying. "I tried edging the ring up when I first examined the body, but the finger is too large."

"A distinguished gentleman like Clive Watney-Banks," Hopkins observed, "wouldn't allow a ring to be so ill-fitting. He would have it re-sized."

"Besides," I added, "bodies tend to shrink in death."

"Quite so," said Holmes. "Now to the more important bit."

Despite any discomfiture on Hopkins' or my part, Sherlock Holmes proceeded to delicately unwrap the burnt thing that once had been a living man's head. Bits of black ash clung to the white silk as Holmes slowly moved the cloth aside and revealed the horror where a human face used to be. Then from his pocket he withdrew a piece of paper and unfolded a small chart.

It presented two horizontal lines of connected boxes—one above the other; a few shaded, most not—which after a moment of confusion I recognised as an elongated representation of teeth depicted in the order in which they appear in the jaw.

"Note the teeth in the chart that are blackened, gentlemen. These mark the seven teeth that Clive's dentist had filled. While the fillings might not last the heat of the flames, the regularity of the drill-work reflects the dentist's skill."

Holmes pointed out the teeth on the chart. Then, to see if the cavities matched, he performed the grisly task of looking into the black, burnt-out hole that was the mouth of the dead man. By this time, of course, there was no expectation that the teeth in the blackened jaw would correspond with those represented in the chart. The ill-fitting ring had prepared me for that conclusion.

"According to the record," Holmes went on, "Clive Watney-Banks had two fillings on the right side of his lower jaw and one on the left. As you can see, if you are so inclined, this corpse has three on the right and two on the left. What is more, attached to two of the corpse's upper teeth is a still-present metal staple, a bridge that appears to be coated in melted porcelain. I have no doubt that the porcelain is the remains of a false-tooth that melted in the fire. A look at this chart reveals that Watney-Banks had no such denture."

"Why, Mr. Holmes," Hopkins exclaimed, "this proves—"

"Quite so, Inspector," Holmes said again. "A check of the dead man's mouth reveals he is not whom we thought him to be."

"Well," Hopkins concluded, "there will be no burial today. I shall make the announcement."

Needless to say, at the same time we had been examining the corpse, the mourners who had come expecting to attend a funeral began raising questions regarding the delay. As Hopkins opened the door, one could hear people asking Olivia about when the procession would begin and her protestations of ignorance.

The appearance of Inspector Hopkins in his long coat and tweeds soon quieted the voices. "I'm afraid," he said, raising his hands, "there will be no funeral today. Further investigative work needs to be done before the body can be laid to rest. I must ask all of you to leave."

Despite renewed bewilderment, the majority of people seemed ready to oblige. A few tried asking Olivia additional questions, but all she could do was shrug. Within minutes most everyone had filed out of the house, and the hearse with its black horses and four pallbearers was sent on its way.

I took the opportunity to ask Holmes where he got the idea to check the teeth?"

"Why, from your friend," he smiled. "It was your Dr. Ottolengui who put me on to it."[*]

Holmes reached into his pocket and produced a cablegram.

I admit I felt a pang of betrayal upon learning that my recently acquired acquaintance had sent the message directly to Holmes and not to me. The cable

---

[*] In a footnote to the Library of Congress Crime Classics edition of Ottolengui's *Final Proof* (2020), Leslie S. Klinger describes a sheriff in Yonkers, New York, who, having read of Ottolengui's faith in forensic dentistry, identified the body of a dead young girl through the examination of her teeth. ("The first fictional use of dental identification," according to Klinger, "was by Joseph Sheridan le Fanu in his 1872 short novel, *The Room in the Dragon Volant*.")

was dated the twenty-fourth of February, the day after the murder, the day the horribly disfigured corpse identified as that of Clive Watney-Banks had been described in the prints, the day that Ottolengui must have first heard the news.

Addressed to Sherlock Holmes, the cable read as follows:

Regarding the corpse found in St. John's Wood: With the face destroyed, positive identification will be difficult. Rely on the teeth. No two people have the same dental services. Patients save their teeth by having them filled. Most dentists keep records.
*--Dr. R. Ottolengui**

It took but a few moments for me to appreciate that much more was at stake than my hurt feelings over being bypassed. There was still a crime to solve, and I could take comfort in recalling that in one of his letters to me, Ottolengui had written that his knowledge of Holmes' reputation was due in large part to my sketches.

---

* For a more complete presentation of Dr. Ottolengui's argument, see his novella, *The Phoenix of Crime*, published in 1898 and reproduced in the aforementioned *Final Proof*. In it, Ottolengui wrote, "We find the people habitually saving their teeth by having them filled. . . . It is a common practice among dentists to register in a book of record all work done for a patient. In these records they have blank charts of the teeth, and on the diagram of each tooth, as it is filled, they mark in ink the size and position of the filling inserted. . . . Members of the dental profession have long urged upon the police the reliance that may be placed upon the dentist in identifying living criminals or unknown dead bodies."

Ready to contribute, I told Holmes, "Now I understand your question to Olivia about Watney-Banks' dentist. At first, I thought it had something to do with your own teeth."

"Good old Watson," Holmes smiled. "Worrying over your friend's health. No, I went to Dr. Davies' office yesterday afternoon to shed light on this case. Miss Watney-Banks was most helpful in granting me access."

"Is it from Dr. Davies that you got the chart then?" I asked.

"Indeed. Ottolengui was quite right about dental record-keeping. Dr. Davies did have information about Watney-Banks' teeth, and he was kind enough—when I informed him of the murder investigation—to provide me with the appropriate chart."

Through the open doorway we could see Hopkins in the sitting room explaining to Olivia and Charles what we had discovered—that the dead man was not Clive Watney-Banks, that Olivia's uncle and Charles' father was alive somewhere. The two cousins took each other's hands. Expressions of surprise, joy, and—dare I say—fear appeared upon their faces.

Leaving them to their familial embrace, Hopkins returned to the library. "Quite fortunate that we got here in time to stop the funeral, eh, Mr. Holmes?"

"Quite so," said Holmes. "I myself was actually delayed a bit before I got to the Yard."

"Delayed this morning?" I asked. "I for one wondered what happened after you left here yesterday afternoon and didn't return."

"In a word, I was followed."

"By whom?" I wanted to know.

"Not this case, Watson. The other one, the one involving Scotland Yard. Hopkins is aware. No need to worry."

Once more I was being put off. But a glance at the two cousins in the sitting room reminded me that more pressing matters were at hand. Once again, I asked Holmes about the preceding afternoon.

"As it turns out," he said, "Dr. Davies' office is not far from Baker Street, and—by Jove, man—I wanted to spend the night in familiar digs. It was my plan to awaken early this morning and walk along the canal until I located the *Marvel*, the boat where Olivia told us Roland Frothingham was squatting."

"Alone, Holmes? You were going to walk alone—with all your concerns?"

"You're right to worry, Watson. It was indeed a capital blunder to stop at 221B. My rooms were being watched, you see. It was still dark this morning when I left, but within minutes I noted a man in black who was trailing after me. He followed me along the Outer Circle past Regent's Park on the way to the canal.

"When I reached the water at the Maida Hill Tunnel, it remained quite dark. There are few gas lamps along the edge and enough foliage despite the cold to create the feel of menace. A heavy mist and malodorous smell were coming off the water. The coots, the moorhens, the geese—they were still asleep. Save for the lapping of the turbid water, all was silent—no doubt the reason I could hear so clearly the fast-approaching footsteps some distance behind me.

"I required but a moment to clamber over the low fence-railing by the canal, step backward a few paces, and crouch down to await my pursuer. In the lingering darkness, he would never be able to see me.

"After a minute or so, he too climbed over the railing, a tall man working hard, his breath clouding up in the damp air. With his back to me, it was mere child's play to grab him by the ankle, give a tug, and send him tumbling over the edge into the murky water."

"Well done, Holmes," I said.

"There was lots of shouting and thrashing from below, but I paid it no mind. Couldn't be bothered. The canal is not so deep that the miscreant couldn't stand up—that is, if the sludge and silt at the bottom allowed him purchase."

"And there are the escape ramps," offered Hopkins, "the inclines that lead to the towpath in case a tow-horse falls into the water."

"In any case," said Holmes, "I was no longer worried about the fellow. In this cold weather, running about in wet clothes does not lend itself to continuing the hunt."

I was about to ask Holmes if he had found the boat, but Hopkins had a more pressing question.

"If not Watney-Banks, Mr. Holmes, whose corpse were we just about to bury?"

"Yes, that is indeed the question, Hopkins. We have the body of an unknown individual, and there must be someone who knows whose body it is. Somewhere there must be a person who is unaccounted for, which is why I asked you for a list of the missing people reported to the Metropolitan Police in the last few days, along with the names of those who reported them missing."

"Ah yes," said Hopkins, "the list." He reached inside his coat pocket and handed Holmes a sheet of paper containing a number of names and family relationships.

Holmes held up the page and muttered as he scanned the column: "A missing son, a missing wife, a missing daughter, a missing husband. A missing husband," he repeated, "a husband reported missing by one Céline Roux, a French woman visiting from Plymouth. Missing since Sunday." Holmes read this last entry more closely. "I am disappointed, Hopkins," he said upon looking up. "You are usually more thorough. In this case, however, it is clear that you have not examined the listings."

"That's right, Mr. Holmes," Hopkins admitted. "I do have other cases that concern me. I just had time to collect the paper from one of our clerks. How did you know I haven't read it?"

Holmes smiled and pointed a finger at Hopkins. "Because, Inspector, had you in fact read the list, you would have discovered that the surname of the French woman's husband is Frothingham."

Chapter Nine

Identities Revealed

Now a man with two names
is usually a crook,
to my way of thinkin'.
--Rodrigues Ottolengui
The Phoenix of Crime

With the funeral no longer scheduled for Friday, Inspector Hopkins returned to Scotland Yard for an official investigation into missing persons. It was clear that he was leaving to Sherlock Holmes the opportunity to communicate with the French woman who had reported the absence of her husband. After checking yet again that no one was pursuing us, Holmes hailed a hansom, and we drove the two miles from St. John's Wood to the Langham Hotel in the West End where the police file reported Céline Roux as staying.

Sheathed in honey-coloured Portland Stone, the Langham is a stately establishment whose large lobby offers a number of nooks in which to have a modicum of privacy on the plushest of couches and chairs. The clerk at the desk secured a hotel page with whom we could send a message to the lady we were seeking, and within five minutes she met us at the desk.

Céline Roux was attired in a dress of purple velveteen, a cream-coloured mantle draped over her shoulders. Her black hair hung in ringlets, and her dark eyes flashed when she saw us. She was clearly French though I was relieved to discover that she spoke perfect English. (My attentive readers will forgive me for not attempting to recreate her accent though I repeat a few key words to authenticate our discussion.)

"You have news of my husband?" she asked once we introduced ourselves.

"*Nous verrons*," said Holmes. "If you can answer some questions for us."

"*Oui,*" she said, "I try."

"You reported to the police that your husband is Arthur Frothingham. And yet your own surname is different. Why is that?"

"It is a long story, I am afraid, *monsieur*. And I do not see how it affects his disappearance."

"Let me be the judge of that," said Holmes. "You see, in addition to finding your husband, we are here to clear an innocent person charged with a crime—a young man called Roland Frothingham. With the same surname as your husband, one suspects they are related."

"I know the name," she said. "I have seen it in the newspapers, but it means nothing to me. This Roland—he is the son of a cousin of my husband. He is a—a *parent éloigné*—what you English call a 'distant relative.' Arthur and I have been married for fifteen years, and we have never met him—though I shed no tears for the swine he is charged with killing."

"You recognise the name of the victim then, Clive Watney-Banks?"

"Watney-Banks," the woman sneered. "I spit on the name. That family is the cause of all our troubles."

"How so?" Holmes asked.

"I met my husband sixteen years ago in Paris. He was working for your government there. We got along, and we married. Not long thereafter, a conniving woman named Jane Watney-Banks came with her young daughter and her brother, Clive, to see Arthur. *Zut alors!* They told us that their parents were dead—that they had no one else to help each other but themselves in this matter."

"And what matter was that?" I asked.

"This vile woman actually claimed to be married to Arthur—falsely claimed that *she* was the wife of my husband. But, you see, this fabrication was nothing new. Arthur had already told me no such marriage ever took place.

"This woman—she had the nerve to call herself Jane *Frothingham* though her true surname, as I have said, was Watney-Banks—this woman had been a nurse in Oxford. She took care of Arthur, who had been injured in a carriage accident during his student days. Though he was from the upper-class and she was not, Arthur told me how Jane Watney-Banks had seduced him into what we French call *l'union libre*. Ultimately, he gave in to her entreaties and agreed to marry her.

"Arthur's father, Sir William Frothingham, a baronet in London, was not as easily duped as my poor Arthur. Sir William was outraged that his son had any sort of relationship with an immoral commoner and ordered Arthur to leave her before any such wedding could take place. My husband saw the wisdom in his father's words and did. With her plans falling apart, the woman was devastated, and only later did she discover she was *enceinte*—pregnant—a little girl, it turned out. This child—Olivia—this child was Arthur's daughter— or so the witch claimed.

"Of course, I never believed her—her—how do you say?—her *mensonge insidieux*—"

"Insidious lie," said Holmes.

"*Exactement*—her 'insidious lie'—*two* lies I suspect—that she and Arthur had married and that the

117

child was their daughter. She claimed that Arthur had turned his back to them, and Jane—too proud to beg, I suppose—raised the little girl on her own. But once that schemer read in the newspapers that, thanks to his father's connections, Arthur had been given a government position in Paris, she was determined to get him back. She believed that once he saw the five-year-old girl—a so-called daughter whom he didn't even know about—he'd have a change of heart, and the family could reunite. To win Arthur back, she gave him a locket. Oh, he's shown it to me. It contained a likeness of the little girl. The cover had even been engraved *JF to AF*."

Jane Frothingham to Arthur Frothingham, I thought. This was the locket that had been displayed at the inquest, the one stolen from Olivia by Roland Frothingham and found clutched in the hand of the yet-to-be-identified dead man.

"Arthur denounced these absurd claims of marriage, but the woman—this *putain*—along with her brother, would not give up her ridiculous fantasies and took her accusations to the *cour d'assises*. Oh, the two of them—she and Clive—came well-prepared to defend their lies. They produced a wedding licence—forged, of course. And yet—if you can believe it—they convinced the magistrate that Jane and my husband had been legally married. They succeeded in having our own marriage—how do you say?—*annulé*."

"Nullified, annulled," Holmes offered.

"*Oui*, 'annulled.' For this so-called crime, I had only to resume the surname of Roux, but Arthur—Arthur was gaoled in Paris for three months—not a terribly harsh sentence, perhaps, but unfair just the same, and long enough to ruin his growing career in France."

Justifiably gaoled, I thought, *because Jane Watney-Banks' charges against the man were accurate— not the lies with which Arthur Frothingham had tried to convince Céline Roux.*

"What was Arthur's reaction to what he claimed was so obviously a miscarriage of justice?" Holmes asked.

"What do you think? Our marriage ruined! His career ended! He was furious. For three months in gaol his anger had time to fester, and when he came out, he vowed revenge. 'I shall return to England,' he told me, 'and I shall destroy the two of them—Jane and her scheming brother.' Not long after he was released, however, we learned that the witch had died—a just end to her duplicitous plot. Her brother Clive, who blamed his sister's death on the grief caused by Arthur, was now left on his own to raise the girl."

"Clive's niece, you mean," I pointed out.

"His *fille adoptive*, as I understand it," the French woman said. "In any case, following his legal troubles, Arthur wanted to return to England, and we moved to Plymouth. It's a port city, so we can sail to France whenever we want without any trouble. I hoped the death of Jane would lessen Arthur's desire for vengeance, and as the years passed, he spoke less and less of his murderous intent. I hoped he was finished.

"But then he read an announcement in the *Times* about the coming-of-age celebration of Olivia. However little he wanted to admit it, I think Arthur came to believe that in spite of his disdain for the woman who had claimed to be his wife, the child really must have been his daughter. He had mellowed over the years, and he vowed to go to London to introduce himself to her."

The more I listened, the more I could not fathom that this French woman saw no relationship between the facts she was relating and the fate of the missing Arthur Frothingham. "You do not think, Madam," I asked in disbelief, "that this story you are telling is connected to the disappearance of your husband?"

She responded with a Gallic shrug.

"What next?" Holmes prodded.

Céline Roux took a deep breath and resumed her account. "Though Arthur had come to accept the idea of having a daughter, he could not rid himself of his rage at the person who had ruined his life. I tried, but could not dissuade him. The girl was twenty-one and no longer in need of her uncle's stewardship. According to Arthur, it was time to put an end to Clive Watney-Banks once and for all. I begged him not to go. But on Saturday, thinking I still might have a chance to change his mind, I travelled by train with him to London. We registered here at the Langham.

"After Sunday dinner, he told me to stay in our suite, for he believed it would be awkward for me to be there when he met his now-grown daughter. Again, I begged him not to go, but he said he had to settle the matter with Clive. As I reported to the police, Sunday evening was the last time I saw him."

"What does your husband look like?" Holmes asked. "How was he dressed on Sunday?"

She smiled ruefully. "He is most proud of his thick black beard. It covers some facial scars from the carriage accident in Oxford, so he'll never remove it. It was cold on Sunday, and he wore his brown-felt slouch hat and his warm ulster. Here," she said, opening her reticule, "I have a *carte de visite*." She handed Holmes the picture-card that confirmed her description.

Holmes looked at me and cocked an eyebrow. I knew what he was thinking. The photographic image very much matched the description of the mysterious

Sunday-night stranger offered by the station-master in St. John's Wood Road. To me, I might add, the image also bore a resemblance to the Clive Watney-Banks I had seen from a distance at Sunday's *fête*.

"One last question, Madam," said Holmes. "Was your husband missing a tooth?"

"*Mais oui*," she answered, "yes," her eyes widening as the tragic implication of Holmes' question penetrated her thinking.

"Do you know where my husband is, Mr. Holmes?" the woman asked quietly. "Is he alive?"

"I have an idea," said Holmes, "but since I am not yet certain, I can't answer either of your questions just now." Turning to me, he added, "Come, Watson. These are deep waters. We must return to Woodlawn House."

Holmes thanked Céline Roux for her help and promised to inform her of any developments concerning the missing Arthur Frothingham.

A doorman dressed in plush grey livery secured us a hansom.

The drive back to St. John's Wood allowed me the opportunity to think about matters. One might logically conclude that the frustration at being denied the woman he loved had turned young Roland Frothingham into a murderer. Yet according to what we had just discovered from the dental records, we now had to ask, 'the murderer of whom?' Surely not Clive Watney-Banks.

Arthur Frothingham, perhaps? But the latter was a member of Roland's own family. What possible reason could Roland have for eliminating a relative? Then again, however illogical a motive might appear, there still remained that pistol we had discovered under the ceramic tile in the cottage where Roland had presumably left it. I said as much to Holmes.

My friend shook his head. "Roland Frothingham didn't go back to his family's cottage the night of the murder. Remember that after leaving Woodlawn, he was discovered in Dover."

Suddenly, I recalled the strange noises I had heard during our first night at Woodlawn—the bumps, the thuds. *Might they have come from some secret place in the house?* I wondered. In any case, it was time to report the phenomenon.

Holmes cocked an eyebrow. "You thought such activity not worth mentioning?" Shaking his head, he added, "Dear Watson, you listen, but you do not hear." For the remainder of the drive back to St. John's Wood, Holmes sat with his eyes closed and his voice silent.

When we arrived in Woodlawn House, we were greeted by Olivia. She was seated on a couch in the sitting room and stood when we entered.

"Are you closer to finding out who the dead man is," Olivia asked, "the man we almost buried?"

"We are indeed," answered Holmes. "We met a woman who reported her husband missing, and we have every reason to believe we've identified the body mistaken for your uncle's."

"Who was he, Mr. Holmes?" Olivia asked. "I must know."

"We all want to know," I said.

"You don't understand," she countered, furrowing her brow. "You see, I believe I'm partly to blame for concealing the man's killer."

Holmes and I both stared at the woman.

A picture of distress, she ran her fingers through her yellow hair. "I have a confession to make," she whispered, blinking back tears.

"Please, sit down," I said, helping her return to the couch. "You look upset."

Holmes and I took seats in the wing chairs opposite. "Now what is this confession?" Holmes asked, his eyes sharp in anticipation.

"I helped my uncle with his elaborate *charade*," Olivia said quietly.

"*Charade*?" I echoed.

"Yes. You see, when I returned to the house from my meeting with Roland at the boat, I discovered my uncle in a strange disguise—ginger-haired and clean-shaven. To be honest, I didn't recognise him at first."

"Quite the dramatic discovery," I remarked.

"Indeed, Doctor, but nothing compared to the smell in the house."

"Burning flesh," Holmes said.

"I rushed into the library and saw the poor man in the fire. It was just awful.

"'He's dead,' my uncle told me as he led me out of the room. 'There's nothing to be done.'

"'Who is he?' I demanded to know. 'What happened to your hair and your beard? What have you done?'

"But my uncle didn't tell me much. He said that the man had come here to kill him and that my uncle had shot him in self-defence."

"And you believed him?" I asked.

"Yes. You see, he said it had something to do with my mother a long time ago, and—oh, he never really made it clear to me. He said he'd been anticipating such a confrontation for many years. What's more, he felt certain that if I cooperated with him, we could pass the dead man off as himself—as Clive Watney-Banks—and save my uncle from arrest. He was so convincing that I went along with his ruse."

"By ruse," said Holmes, "I assume you mean by accepting him as your cousin."

"But the difference in your ages," I said. "Surely—"

Olivia forced a laugh. "Oh, I didn't really believe we could do it. He's twenty years older than I, but he does look much younger without his beard. Besides, it was worth the risk. I had a chance to protect my uncle, and the other man was already dead."

"We believe," said Holmes drily, "that the 'other man,' as you put it, was called Arthur Frothingham."

"Frothingham?" she repeated with a frown.

Clearly, this "Arthur" was a Frothingham she did not recognise.

"Is there a connection between this Arthur and Rollo?" she wanted to know.

"Distant relatives," Holmes replied, "but nothing more—at least, as far as we have ascertained. Apparently, Arthur Frothingham had a long-lasting feud with your family."

That the man might also have been the young woman's father Holmes neglected to mention.

Olivia crossed her arms. "I was mad to have helped my uncle. I realise that now. But he has been like a father to me."

"As I am certain you must realise, Miss Watney-Banks," said Holmes, "in addition to your own concerns, there is a woman agonising over the disappearance of Arthur Frothingham as we speak, and whatever we think of either him or your uncle, we must find your uncle and let the law decide who was right."

"I see that now," she agreed.

"Do you know where he is?" Holmes asked.

She shook her head. "After breakfast he went to his room, but I haven't seen him leave."

"We suspect," said Holmes, "that someone might still be lurking on the grounds or perhaps"—here he looked at me askance—"somewhere inside the house itself. Watson has told me of hearing strange sounds in the middle of the night."

"Is there an attic?" I asked.

"No," Olivia replied.

Holmes shook his head. "There's no space for an attic, Watson. You forget the flat roof. And yet, though all the rooms on the ground floor are the same size, their closets produce a narrowed hallway whilst the rooms on the first floor have only armoires—"

"But there is still a narrow hallway up there!" I exclaimed. At last, I understood. "Good gracious, Holmes, there must be a secret room taking up the space on the first floor—like a priest hole."

"A secret room," repeated Olivia slowly. "I never knew of such a thing . . . . How could I have been so blind?"

I now remembered the door on the ground floor in front of which I had spent the first night at Woodlawn. "Try Charles' room. He managed to get out when no exit was apparent."

Holmes followed my suggestion. He knocked on the door, received no answer, and entered. With Charles nowhere to be seen, Holmes began searching for some sort of entrance to a hiding space. He tried moving bookcases and touching with his long fingers the tops of various pieces of furniture and wall mouldings—but to no avail.

Then Holmes opened the door to the closet. Olivia and I were standing well behind him, but immediately all three of us sprang back. Framed by the hanging clothes that had been pushed to either side, Hengist the mastiff lay curled on the floor and raised his head when the door swung open. The great dog recognised Olivia and whimpered softly as he lowered his head once more.

Olivia called the dog, and with a plaintive cry Hengist rose and lumbered over to her. But then he turned and shambled back to the closet and, looking upward, began to howl.

Olivia walked him to the other side of the room, and the mastiff curled at her feet and whimpered again.

"Something terrible is bothering him," she said.

The closet itself was dark, but pushing aside more clothes, Holmes looked to the ceiling. "There's a trap door," he reported. "Get me a chair."

"A secret room," murmured Olivia once again. "I had no idea."

A Windsor bow back stood against the rear wall, and I offered it to Holmes, who placed it beneath the trap door. Climbing upon the seat, he pushed upward, and silently the trap door moved. Holmes slid it aside and hoisted himself into the space above.

No sooner did his feet disappear than he shouted, "It's dark as pitch in here." The words were muffled by his confinement, and I moved closer to the open trap to hear more clearly. It was then that I detected the scratch of a Vesta on its striker, and a flare of match-flame momentarily illuminated the small area visible beyond the trap.

"What do you see up there, Mr. Holmes?" Olivia asked.

"There's a small ladder lying next to the trap. It must be used for climbing in and out. There's also a lamp."

A moment later, the background brightened, and we listened to his movements as he searched the area above us. It took but a minute or two before he announced his grim discovery: "There's a body in here. I am afraid, Miss Watney-Banks, it is that of your uncle."

The young woman said nothing in response. She simply joined me in watching
the feet of the ladder emerge through the trap. I moved the chair to the side, and Holmes lowered the ladder to the floor. Then, carefully directing his feet onto the top rung, he climbed down and turned toward Olivia. "Judging from the small bottle of cyanide next to him, I'd say that Clive Watney-Banks has taken his own life."

Chapter Ten

The Confession

We have once more
an evidence of the futility
of planning a crime
which shall leave no clue behind.
                    --Rodrigues Ottolengui
                    "The Missing Link"

"Your uncle left his change of costumes up there—mainly, his sea clothes—along with his make-up and a collection of false beards. There's hair dye and a wash basin as well. It's where he transformed himself from father to son."

Olivia simply shook her head.

"I had only a short time to look about up there," said Sherlock Holmes, "but it was as you told us, Miss Watney-Banks. There are so many provisions that your uncle must have been planning this scheme for some time. There's the poison, of course, but water, bread and cheese as well.

"The room itself is long and narrow. Still, there's sufficient space for a small bed, a chair, and a writing table complete with paper, pen and ink. I brought some pages down. From the little I read, they appear to contain your uncle's confession."

Holmes reached inside his coat and produced a bundle of folded papers. When he opened the sheets, I could see they were covered in neat penmanship, the same careful handwriting I remembered from the fictional letters the false Charles had shown us supposedly sent to him by his father.

Olivia, eager to see the pages, took a step towards Holmes.

"First," he said, "we must notify the police." Still clutching the bundle in one hand, he walked down the hallway to the outer door and stepping outside beneath the cupola, produced his silver police whistle and blew into it.

Within minutes a constable arrived and, touching his forelock to signal his understanding of Holmes' request, went off to summon Inspector Hopkins. Only then did we take our places in the sitting room to hear Holmes read aloud the final words of Olivia's uncle.

Intended for whoever finds this first [Watney-Banks had written]—*though I put my money on Sherlock Holmes:*

To my unbridled dismay, my plans have miscarried. Years of careful plotting have resulted in my downfall. I answer to my misdeeds with my life.

The horror began the weekend of my lovely Olivia's majority. What should have been a time of celebration turned sour when Olivia's beau, Roland Frothingham, sought my approval to marry her. I had no idea they were so involved with each other— have been for many years. I did not see the warning signs. I should have put him out when I first learned his surname, when I realised that he was a member of Arthur Frothingham's family. As it was, I blurted too much of the truth at the garden party when I impugned his family name.

A brief history: Although Olivia doesn't know it yet, Arthur Frothingham was her father. My sister Jane—Olivia's dear mother as well as Frothingham's wife—was a nurse, an angel of mercy, the kindest person in the world—and the rogue left her before Olivia's birth in 1870.

Five years later, now living in Paris, the blackguard tried to marry another woman. But Jane—who (much to my astonishment) still had feelings for the cad—intended to put a stop to it.

My own sweet wife, whom I had met and married in Oxford, died from smallpox not long thereafter. Alone that I was after university, I moved to a flat in Hampstead to ponder my future. Thus, it happened that I had no major commitments and could travel with my sister and little Olivia to Paris when Jane decided to set matters right with her husband.

Thanks to the French courts, Jane won her case against Arthur Frothingham. His "new" marriage was annulled, and he was sentenced to prison. Oh, justice may have been served right enough, but the man himself swore vengeance, vowing to kill both my sister and me.

Jane avoided such an end, however, dying the following year from what I believe was the consequence of her exhaustive efforts to right the wrongs perpetrated against her by her husband.

And yet to think that Olivia, Jane's lovely daughter, now desires to marry into that deceitful family!

Which brings me to the present. A few days before the fateful garden party celebrating Olivia's majority, I received a note from the villain himself. The message read simply: Sunday night. *It was signed,* Arthur Frothingham.

But I was ready.

Ever since Frothingham had made the threat some fifteen years before, I had engineered a plan not only to stop him cold, but also to effect his destruction under the cover of impunity.

To implement my plan, I drew from my inheritance to facilitate the move from Hampstead to Woodlawn House. I was twenty-six at the time and— thanks to the stage make-up plus the dye in my ginger-hair and newly-grown beard—not only looked considerably older but also—as was my plan—greatly resembled Arthur Frothingham. What's more, due to my association with the entomologist, George Hampson, whom I'd met through common friends at Oxford after I'd graduated, I secured a respectable position at the Museum of Natural History.

Next, I invented a make-believe son. I named him Charles, and I enrolled him at Bedford House Church School in Oxford. It is an establishment with which I am familiar because it had just opened during my days at university there. I travelled to Oxford under the pretence of evaluating the school in preparation for its reception of my non-existent son.

To confirm the lad's reality, I took rooms there for a month and arranged for letters that I, the father, had previously written to be sent to 'C. Watney-Banks,' the son, in Oxford. They were, of course, delivered to me, and to prove that Charles had attended Bedford House, I displayed to Sherlock Holmes the spurious letters I had an ignorant associate post to me all those years ago.

After preparing the school's administrators to receive the boy, I informed Mr. Thorogood, the principal, that to my great distress, my wilful, thirteen-year-old son had run off and somehow secured a role as cabin boy on a ship in the Merchant Navy.

But all that was years ago. Let me return to the hours following my niece's party on Sunday. As a result of that note from Arthur Frothingham which I had got a few days earlier, I remained on edge. Alone in the house late Sunday evening, I awaited my nemesis.

Suddenly loud barking and growling caught my attention—it must be Arthur, I assumed, who had aroused my dog—unless, of course, it was that other Frothingham, Roland, out to complete the murder he had attempted earlier in the garden. Either way, when a bullet penetrated the window of the library and lodged in the ceiling, I was sure one or the other of them had come to complete his revenge.

I grabbed Olivia's pistol, which she had left on the mantel, and fired blindly into the darkness without success. Another shot came from outside, but it went wild and missed the house entirely. In the end, whoever had been fighting with Hengist disappeared, and I sat down to calm myself.

Within minutes, however, I heard knocking at the outer door. I reckoned that one of the Frothinghams, Arthur or Roland, had succeeded in eluding the dog and reached the house. To avoid incriminating Olivia, I replaced her gun on the mantel and chose instead, knowing it still contained most of its bullets, the pistol I had stored in my desk, the same pistol I had picked up from the ground at the garden party—the pistol belonging to Roland Frothingham.

I opened the outer door and beheld my antagonist from so many years before—Arthur Frothingham. Though a trifle stouter than I remembered him, we appeared, as I had hoped, the mirror image of each other—my black beard and black hair mimicking his own. "Watney-Banks," he greeted me. Then he turned sideways, and immediately made a quick move with his hand to his pocket.

Fearing a gun that would end my own life, I shot the man dead and initiated my years-old plan. I dragged the body to the bedroom and stripped it, paying special attention to the coat and shirt containing the hole made by my bullet. I then clothed it in my own monogramed night-dress and forced my wedding ring as far as I could onto the *thick finger of the corpse. I smeared blood from the wound onto the night-dress, but when I realised the night-dress lacked a bullet hole, I shot through the cloth to make it look like the dead man had been wearing it when struck. To make it appear as if he had been hit only once, I attempted to hit the same spot as the shot that killed him. Though the bullet passed through his body, I missed the first wound by an inch or so. There should be a bullet hole somewhere in the bedroom floor as the result of my poorly aimed endeavour.*

To complete the staging, I dragged the body to the library, maneuvered its head into the fireplace, and roasted the villain's face beyond recognition. Once I completed that gruesome task, which included cleaning up the excess blood, I climbed through the trap to my secret room on the first floor, a hide I had constructed many years ago as part of my plan for revenge.

I shaved my beard and washed out the black dye from my hair. Frothingham's slouch hat would cover my red locks, and I applied the false black beard I'd saved for the occasion, employing a scissors to shape it more like Frothingham's. At last, I donned my seaman's clothing, which I concealed beneath the dead man's ulster I had put on. I filled a grip with the rest of his clothes—including his shirt and jacket that retained the hole from the bullet I had shot into him. Finally, I added Roland's pistol.

At that moment, I heard Olivia returning. She entered through a French window. Confronting me in my disguise was awkward enough, but the burning corpse and the stink in the house could not be explained away. I had to tell her what had happened and convince her my actions were to protect my own life.

So strongly did I hate the Frothingham name, however, that not even my love for Olivia could dissuade me from leaving her beloved Roland culpable. I successfully coerced her to go along with my scheme whilst at the same time remaining careful not to inform her of my plan to implicate her beau. Noble young innocent that Olivia is, she agreed to accept me in the role of her invented cousin.

After telling Olivia I would return the next day as the imaginary Charles, I placed the dead man's slouch hat on my head and checked that the false beard was secure. Finally, disguised as the bewhiskered stranger who had arrived at the station a few hours earlier, I left by train for West Hampstead where Olivia had previously told me Roland's cottage was located.

Once I assured myself that the cottage was empty, I dropped the dead man's clothes and my false beard into the fireplace and set them ablaze. I loosened a tile in the kitchen floor and dug a small hole in which I placed the pistol bearing Roland's name. Leaving a bit of tile raised, I reasoned it would not be difficult for the police to find the gun. All I had left to do was return to Woodlawn the next day and appear in the sea-faring guise of my red-headed, clean-shaven son Charles.

When I did so, however, I was shocked to see how quickly Sherlock Holmes had joined the investigation. Not that his appearance spelled doom for my plan. But it did impel me to see the possible need for setting these words down on paper should I need to explain myself.

In retrospect, I should have anticipated that in order to clear himself of the murder-charge, Roland would have to rely on my beloved Olivia as his alibi. To my great consternation, I realised that if I don't admit my murderous deed, my clever machinations will result in my adoptive daughter's being named an accomplice in the killing of her real father. I cannot let such an outcome remain a possibility. She is innocent of all wrong-doing. I trust this confession and my subsequent death will clear her of any blame. I can only pray for her forgiveness.

Clive Watney-Banks
27 February, 1891

"My father? Olivia gasped when Holmes had finished reading her uncle's revelations. Until then, she had sat silently taking in all the details. "Arthur Frothingham was my father? I—I had no idea. Oh," she groaned putting her head in her hands, "how much more terrible it all is."

As if to comfort her, the dog laid his head in her lap, and I suddenly realised why the animal had been so friendly towards Charles. "Why, Hengist recognised Charles as Clive from the start."

"The curious incident of the dog who showed us the truth, eh, Watson?" said Holmes.

"If we were only smart enough to understand it."

Olivia stroked the dog's head. "At least my uncle's confession clears Rollo of any blame. The police will have to let him go now. Of that I can be truly thankful."

"But the locket," I found myself saying. "Though your uncle's admissions may explain the strange noises I heard Monday night, they do not resolve how the locket that had been in Roland's possession had got into the dead man's hand. As much as I hate to point it out, regardless of your uncle's disclosures, I believe that the locket, which places Roland at the scene of the murder, continues to raise the possibility of his guilt."

"Be not too hasty in your rush to judgement, old fellow," cautioned Holmes. "Remember that Clive Watney-Banks didn't see the locket in Arthur Frothingham's hand. Recall that he believed his victim was reaching for a gun."

"Yes, yes," I replied, "but how does that exonerate Roland?"

"Because, friend Watson," Holmes said, putting his hand inside his coat, "there are, in fact, two lockets." At the same time, he spoke the words, Holmes revealed in his open palm a golden locket that looked identical to the one found in the dead man's hand, the locket we had seen at the inquest.

"Two?" Olivia and I exclaimed at the same time.

"Where did you find this second one?" she asked.

"In the boat that you told me about, Miss Watney-Banks. It was why I went to the canal yesterday—when I was followed, Watson, as I've already told you."

"Followed by whom?" Olivia asked.

"Another case," I told her authoritatively—although in truth I knew next to nothing about the larger investigation involving Scotland Yard in which my friend was participating.

"In any event," Holmes continued, "when I arrived at the Macclesfield Bridge, I found the boat just where you told us, Miss Watney-Banks. Light was beginning to break, and beyond some weeping willows I saw it."

"The canal boat?" I asked.

"Indeed, though given its mere seven-foot width, I should imagine that the *Marvel* is officially considered a 'narrow boat.' Still, there it was—wide enough to contain a cramped cabin aft for the bargeman with a little chimney on the roof and the name *Gardner Brothers,* the coal merchants, painted in red on the outside walls."

"That's the one," Olivia said. "Green with red trim. I met Roland on the deck Sunday night."

"Well," Holmes continued, "I climbed aboard, ducked my head, and entered the cabin. It was empty, but the air was very close. Within the tiny space I saw a stove, a kettle, plates, and a bed—all intricately laid out. In fact, it was on the bed that I found a short, navy-blue jacket rolled into a ball."

"It must have been Roland's," said Olivia. "He's never liked that jacket. It's too tight."

"Tight or not is beside the point," said Holmes. "It's what I found *inside* the jacket that's significant. In a pocket I discovered this little trinket." Holding up the locket again, he gave it a jiggle, then opened it, and showed Olivia the miniature portrait of herself as a child.

"I don't understand," she said.

"There are in reality two lockets," Holmes explained, "both alike in appearance, both alike in content: each containing a picture of *you* as a little girl,

Miss Watney-Banks.   But here's the rub—the two engravings differ slightly.

"With the intent of winning back her husband, your mother Jane gave a gift to Arthur—the locket we saw at the inquest—the one with the letters *JF to AF* engraved on the outside. It was the locket he brought with him from Paris all those years ago.

"But to her little daughter—you—she gave the simple *JF+AF* to represent *both* your parents. It was this second locket, the one given to *you*, Miss Watney-Banks, that was taken from you by Roland and placed in the pocket of the coat he'd left in the *Marvel*."

"But why," Olivia asked, "was the other locket in the hand of the dead man—in the hand of my . . . my father?"

"One can only speculate," said Holmes, obviously relying on Céline Roux's story for a sanguine interpretation. "It has been suggested that your coming-of-age mellowed Arthur and that as a result he sought some sort of reconciliation with both you and your uncle. In his confession, Clive admitted that he thought the man he met at the door Sunday night was reaching for a gun; perhaps, your father was simply reaching for the locket as an appeal to settle their differences. It must have already been in his hand when he was struck by the fatal bullet."

In light of the horrible murder, Holmes had presented a heartening story, and Olivia sat silently absorbing the details.

Minutes later, Inspector Hopkins arrived. Handing him the pages whose contents we had just heard, Holmes alerted him to the suicide in the secret room and, placing special emphasis on Olivia's innocence, summarised the contents of the man's confession.

"If all is as it appears, Mr. Holmes," Hopkins replied, "Miss Watney-Banks should suffer no ill consequences, and young Frothingham will be released as soon as possible."

"I'm going to marry Rollo," Olivia Watney-Banks declared, her broad smile a welcome diversion for Holmes and me.

As Hopkins turned towards the hallway, however, his expression remained grim, for he was about to trek to the hidden room and the dead man inside it. Even Hopkins managed a small smile, however, when Holmes and I were about to take our leave and Olivia proclaimed, "I believe I can say with some authority to all of you gentlemen that the Shooters Club of St. John's Wood is no more."

🔍

We returned to Baker Street by way of the Langham, Holmes continuing to survey the roads to be sure we were not being followed as he had been at the Canal. Our stop at the hotel allowed Holmes to inform Céline Roux of the death of her husband and how it appeared that he had been trying to settle his differences with Clive Watney-Banks before her husband had been killed.

Earlier, Holmes had considered such a theory speculation. Let those who have called my friend unfeeling recognise that he was now offering the speculation as fact in order to provide Frothingham's widow with a memory of her husband to cherish.

The second inquest dealing with the death of Clive Watney-Banks generated even more interest than the proceedings that we now know concerned Arthur

Frothingham, and days after that second inquest concluded with the verdict of suicide, Roland Frothingham and Olivia Watney-Banks announced their plans to be married. The wedding is set for early May, and Holmes and I are both invited. Alas, fearing that we shall be involved in matters of our own at that time, we declined the invitation.

All the events that I have reported in this account concluded a week ago. Sherlock Holmes must still travel back to France to complete his assignment for the government there. Upon his return to these islands, which he maintains will be in late April, I expect he will furnish me with more details concerning the grand criminal investigation of which he is a part. Simply put, however, given his unease related to the forces that seek to harm him, I cannot rid myself of the fears I continue to harbour concerning the fate of our upcoming trip.

Postscript
(added in 1896)

*...The major object of fiction is to entertain,
and even though a little instructive lesson
may be deftly interwoven with the plot,
I fear that the modern novel is too highly
spiced with philosophic dissertations.*
--Rodrigues Ottolengui
The Crime of the Century

It took some three years for the tumultuous business between Sherlock Holmes and Professor Moriarty to come to a satisfying conclusion, for—unknown to me in early '91—it had been Moriarty's criminal organization that had continued to plague Holmes during our time in St. John's Wood. The satisfactory resolution of that business, of course, is another story, most all of which I shall detail in a sketch I plan to call "The Adventure of the Empty House."

Yet even as I bemoaned what I believed to be the loss of my dear friend during the early '90s, Dr. Rodrigues Ottolengui, whilst continuing his distinguished career in dentistry, embarked upon his new role as an author of crime fiction. In that capacity, he has produced numerous short stories and novels concerning the misdeeds of criminals and ne'er-do-wells and the successes of those in constant pursuit of justice like his heroes—the professional detective Jack Barnes and the amateur Robert Leroy Mitchel.

In fairness to Ottolengui, he did seek my approval before transforming the factual details of the Watney-Banks tragedy into a compelling fiction rich with his own inventions. Not only did I approve of his project, but as a writer myself, I encouraged him to complete it. *A Conflict of Evidence*, Ottolengui's novel that resulted from the case, demonstrates the freedom that a purveyor of fiction enjoys in contrast to the boundaries which limit the author dedicated to reporting the facts.

In the name of entertainment, Ottolengui invented a variety of elements and complications intended to baffle as well as engage his readers. In the most obvious of changes, he re-titled the Frothingham family "Marvel" (perhaps inspired by the name of the canal boat), and he moved the setting of the story from St. John's Wood in London to New Hampshire in his native United States.

A Conflict of Evidence also contains a plethora of events that never really happened, of deviations that seem arbitrary, and of coincidences that challenge credulity. One recalls from Ottolengui's novel a secreted note that states the suspected name of the killer, a night-time adventure that occurs in freezing weather in wet clothing, and a disruptive rivalry between the two major investigators that threatens the outcome of the mystery's solution. What is more, the machinations of Detective Barnes allow the novel to conclude in a more positive and sentimental manner than did the events in reality.

A number of publications have gone as far as comparing Rodrigues Ottolengui to the distinguished literatus, Arthur Conan Doyle—not only my literary agent, but also a celebrated author. Indeed, his historical novel, *The White Company*, was serialised to great acclaim in *The Cornhill Magazine* at the same time the events in St. John's Wood were transpiring. Though I too appreciate Ottolengui's authorial accomplishments, I deem it much too early in the man's literary career to equate his fiction with that of a master like Conan Doyle—let alone with the writings of a lesser scrivener like myself.

To be honest, I maintain that in fiction or in fact, success depends upon the author's choice of protagonist. It is my judgment that Ottolengui felt it necessary to add all the embellishments that he did in *A Conflict of Evidence* because no matter how perceptive his detective Jack Barnes might appear, Ottolengui recognised that in the end Barnes lacks the investigative talent and skills of my friend and colleague, Mr. Sherlock Holmes.

The astute observer will agree that Jack Barnes—a "Pilkington" agent, no less[*]—displays keen insight, a sharp eye, and a strong sense of justice. Yet I am certain that most readers will also agree that Barnes lacks the encyclopaedic knowledge, the physical dexterity, and the creative thinking possessed by the man who has called himself "the world's first consulting detective."

In the end, the objective reader must disagree with the observation made on 10 January, 1896—not, it must be said, by Ottolengui himself, but by the American periodical, *Oakes Weekly Republican*. "[Ottolengui's] New York detective," the publication wrongly concluded, "is quite as ingenious as the famous Sherlock Holmes."

THE END

---

[*] Presumably, a play on "Pinkerton."

Editor's Notes

For the fictional account of the Watney-Banks investigation reported by Dr. Watson, see Rodrigues Ottolengui's *A Conflict of Evidence* originally published by G.P. Putnam's Son in 1893.

The online *Arthur Conan Doyle Encyclopedia* lists a number of advertisements casting Ottolengui as the "American Conan Doyle."

For more praise of Ottolengui by Ellery Queen than that which appears in the headnote at the front of this volume, see *Queen's Quorum*, pp. 41, 116.
(For additional references to Ellery Queen's comments on Ottolengui, see Douglas Greene's introduction to Ottolengui's *Before the Fact* in *The Battered Silicon Dispatch Box*, www.batteredbox.com as well as Harry B. Weiss' "Rodrigues Ottolengui, 1861-1937" in *Journal of the New York Entomological Society,* Vol. 59, No. 2 (Jun., 1951), pp. 93-98.)

www.ingramcontent.com/pod-product-compliance
Lightning Source LLC
Chambersburg PA
CBHW020645250626
47154CB00008B/2812